ALL THAT COUNTS

ALL THAT COUNTS

Georg M. Oswald

Translated from the German
by Shaun Whiteside

Grove Press New York

Originally published in German by Carl Hanser Verlag Munchen Wein 2000
under the original title *Alles was Zählt*.

Published simultaneously in Canada
Printed in the United States of America

FIRST GROVE PRESS PAPERBACK EDITION

Library of Congress Cataloging-in-Publication Data

Oswald, Georg M., 1963–
 [Alles was zählt. English]
 All that counts / Georg M. Oswald ; translated from the German by Shaun
Whiteside.
  p. cm.
 ISBN 0-8021-3931-0 (pbk.)
 I. Whiteside, Shaun. II. Title.

PT2675.S95 A4513 2001
833'.92—dc21   2001033998

Design by Laura Hammond Hough

Grove Press
841 Broadway
New York, NY 10003

02 03 04 05 06   10 9 8 7 6 5 4 3 2 1

Inside

1

I go to the office every day.

You probably say the same about yourself, if you happen to have a job, but it's true for me because I'm there on Saturdays, too, and Sundays if necessary. I'm deputy manager of the department of foreclosure and liquidation, and I plan to become *manager* of the department of foreclosure and liquidation. That would mean: one hundred thousand a year basic plus bonus plus company car (third-class BMW).

And that would be good.

I wake up, and Marianne, my wife, isn't lying next to me, but her side of the bed is still warm. The weather forecaster appears on the television screen, a little Sony cube. She's beaming, as though something wonderful has just happened to her. My wife likes to switch on the television the minute she wakes up, and then go to the bathroom or the kitchen.

I roll onto my stomach and pull the pillow over my head.

Marianne calls, "You can use the bathroom now. I'm making coffee."

I roll back onto my back and first look at the ceiling, then at the thin, rather dirty cotton curtain over the window. I think, "Yes, I really am one of those people who can get worked up about dirty curtains." I've talked to Marianne about it. She claims that no matter how many times she washes that curtain, it's always dirty again as soon as she hangs it up. It's all because we live on this street. And in any case—she can't help saying this to me—I can shove my dirty curtains up my ass. You probably think that's funny. I don't.

The commuter traffic is already up and about. There's a traffic jam by the lights at the nearest crosswalk. I imagine you and people like you sitting in your cars, still a bit sad because you couldn't stay in bed, but already pissed off with your line manager.

I take a shower, shave, comb my hair, get dressed. I start thinking about the office.

Marianne has cut out ads for apartments and houses from the paper, and describes them to me at the breakfast table. She notices I'm not listening, and asks me what I'm thinking about. It really is that tired old exchange out of the cartoons. "Darling, what are you thinking about?" "The office."

She asked the question, so I give her the answer. I say, "The office."

More to the point, I'm thinking about why Rumenich told me she wanted to talk to me about the Kosiek case. I'm wondering whether it might be some kind of plot that could affect my position, my market value. But it's not anything that really concerns me, it's trivial.

From one second to the next Marianne and I get into a furious argument, because I asked her—in an irritated voice, she claims—when her aunt Olivia was coming to visit. I decide to divorce her, as I always do when we fight. We maintain a hostile silence for a while, but then suddenly we find ourselves back in a normal conversation. It's about real estate again. I've got to go. I say, "I was going to say something else, I've forgotten what. I'll call you."

Don't go thinking that my days begin any worse than yours do. Just be honest, and then I can save my breath on the subject.

I enjoy my daily trip to work. It's long enough to get a clear notion of what's to come, but too short to get bored.

Marianne complains about the area we live in, that it isn't "representative" enough of our income bracket for her. I like it, because what they call "simple" people live here. You can tell the simple people because they're the ones who live in the most complicated circumstances. They're always preoccupied with getting ahold of money. And because they don't have jobs, or don't have well-paid jobs, they're constantly coming up with new and hopeless ways of getting ahold of it. Of course they haven't the first notion about doing business, and they get ripped off by the first shyster who comes their way. Their lives are governed by debts and by the lies they have to invent to get those debts. First rule in my business. You've got debts, you lie. Always.

There's a fitness center on our block. That's what it says on the door, anyway. First of all it used to be run by a Serb who would make Marianne special offers for the use of the machines. He would make those offers in the corridor, on the elevator, in the street, wherever he happened to bump into her. I know one of his former customers. He told me there were always five or six hookers hanging around the bar waiting for customers. When the Serb had figured out that my wife was married—to me—he changed his tactics. Now he would come on like a gentleman, even when I was there, to stress that his intentions were entirely honorable. In the summer, heavily tattooed bikers would sit outside his place. They would sit in the sun, drink beer from cans and gaze devotedly at their chrome motorcycles, which they had parked on the pavement. They were about as interested in fitness as the hookers were. Although maybe the hookers and the bikers belonged together. I've no idea what the Serb had to do with them, he never told me. One morning I met him with two other guys in the elevator, and it looked as though he was having problems. He wasn't at all polite or friendly to me, as he usually was, and he gave me a look as if to say, "If you know what's best for you, you'll keep your trap shut."

A day later the fitness studio was cleared out by the police. My acquaintance said it had something to do with a truckload of undeclared jeans on the Slovene-Italian border, with illegal gambling and, of course, pimping. The Serb had fled. A few days later there was a different sign on the door of the studio, a cardboard sign, written carefully but rather clumsily in red felt pen: VALUED CUSTOMERS! FOR FINANCIAL REASONS WE HAVE TEMPORARILY CLOSED. IN A FEW

WEEKS WE WILL REOPEN FOR FANTASTIC SPECIAL OFFERS! YOURS TRULY, THE FITNESS TEAM. The fantastic special offers never happened, of course, and the Serb never showed up again. His successor, a deep-tanned, muscle-bound moron called Uwe, had a great idea. He opened up a new health center, Ladies Only, so he could make sure he could dedicate himself entirely to his customers.

Right next to Ladies Only is Period Furniture Paradise, in which copies of Louis XVI and plush nineteenth-century German furniture, porcelain man-high fountains for the sitting room, phony antique cutlery, gaudy crystal glasses, and who knows what all else, is offered at hair-raising prices. Marianne says she's never seen a single customer in the shop, and neither have I. I'm willing to bet that the Serb, with all his hookers and bikers and Fantastic Special Offers, never had half so much crap in his place as the invisible owners of this amazing Period Furniture Paradise. It's about money-laundering—dealing in either drugs or guns, I'm sure of that. I know what I'm talking about. I happened to know the man who used to run the shop through my job. It's a company called Furnituro Ltd., currently in bankruptcy proceedings. The directors are nowhere to be found, as is so often the case. But no one in the street, apart from me, knows about that. I've tried to enforce the bankruptcy action. Without success, unfortunately, because the new owner of the shop claims to have nothing to do with Furnituro Ltd.

I'm interested in every single detail of stories like that. It's part of my training, because in my job you learn to extract the important bits of information. Do you know what your neighbors do? Of course you do, you'll say, they've told me. But do you really know? Believe me, you'd never get over the astonishment if you knew how the people next door *really* made their money. And you'd think your debts were nothing if you knew how many *they* had.

2

think I can vaguely remember a time when things were peaceful, when I wasn't pursuing any goals, or when I was pursuing them in a different way, I don't know how to put it. I was more aware of living in the present. Today it's as though I don't feel anything for weeks, not a single sensation that really belongs to me, nothing that I feel as Thomas Schwarz, and yet at the same time I find myself in a state of floating unease. "Floating unease," that's what I call it.

Recently everything's been happening all at the same time. Stress, stress, stress—you know what I'm talking about?

I was describing my trip to work. You'll be familiar with it in some form or another, I'll bet.

Every morning, as I pass next door's garbage cans, I light a cigarette. "Officially" I stopped years ago, but I'm so fired up every morning that I would *die* without a cigarette, on the spot.

A group of adolescents, between sixteen and eighteen or so, come toward me. They go to the technical school next door. They're extraordinarily interesting people. They're all dressed to the nines, very expensively. That's remarkable in itself, because they don't come from the kind of background where there's cash to spare for dressing up. You'd have to assume that a considerable proportion of their parents' income goes toward this gear. Some of them wear American-designer sportswear and have fashionable hairdos. They're the ones who watch MTV and Viva. They believe in pop culture and pay for the feeling of being part of it. The others dress like successful people in American TV series and movies. The boys wear grey pinstripe suits with white shirts and tasteful ties, the girls wear grey or dark blue suits. And they've got severe but stylish hairdos and classically fashionable shoes. Fine so far. What fascinates me is the touchingly vivid way in which these young people express their desire for social recognition. And I really find it oppressive that not one of them will escape the same crappy life in a two-room apartment for which they so bitterly reproach their parents. How do I know that? These kids are going to the technical school, and anyone who does that today is lost. They know that as well as I do. Of course I know you're not supposed to say it out loud, and if one of them manages to be halfway successful, everyone points at him and shouts, "Look! Anyone can do it!" although he's the one who proves that not everyone can do it, that for the nine hundred and ninety-nine others, the dream of happiness is irrevocably a thing of the past, even if they still have a long way to go before they figure it out.

I spend my time with these reflections on my way to the subway, until I pass the immigration office, whose entrance is on the other side of the road. Every morning it's besieged by hundreds of people trying to get in. What can I say? Thank God the entrance is on the other side of the road. The people are standing around for papers, for money. They want to legalize their status. Fine as far as I'm concerned, nothing to do with me, it's not going to get them anywhere, anyway. Of course, if anyone asks me I say, like everybody else does, the immigration problem has to be solved one way or the other. But in fact I don't see it that way. I just see the people who are in already, and the people who want to get in. And it would be a stroke of bad luck if the ones who are already in couldn't keep the next lot out. So what's the problem? A battle for territory, with clearly assigned roles and all the opportunities on one side, none on the other. I hurry to get down the stairs to the subway. I wouldn't like it if one of them got it into his head to switch platforms and talk to me. I wouldn't much like to be confronted with annoying requests, and it wouldn't get them anywhere, anyway.

This first serious depression of the day takes hold of me as I'm riding the puke-stained escalator down through this collection of *vermin* who get up my nose with their bad breath, their unwashed hair, their phenomenally stupid faces, and with no notion of a private sphere. That's how it is. In the New York subway, which I found completely intolerable in this respect, there was something that I did like. It was the posters called POETRY IN MOTION, stuck up in the narrow little advertising spaces above the windows. I remember one of them:

Sir, you are tough and I am tough
But who will write whose epitaph?

Under it was a name: Joseph Brodsky. A Russian emigré and winner of the Nobel Prize for literature, Marianne told me. I liked the way he managed to cram the law underlying every single encounter so casually into two lines, and in a way that would make you laugh.

I look over the shoulder of a small fat woman who smells of sweet perfume and read her evening paper. When she notices, she presses herself slightly to the side and then hunches over the paper so that I can't read it. Good for her!

Suddenly two old farts to the right of me start getting on my nerves. A frail and lanky, white-haired old guy, at least seventy, who looks like he might have been a high jumper, peers over the top of his copy of *Der Spiegel*, down at his companion, who is a good two heads shorter and not a bit younger.

He's getting worked up about—what else—the penal system. Lots of old men have some inexplicable passion about the penal system. Have you noticed? Unfortunately they're the only ones who know how to improve it: the reintroduction of the death penalty, the stocks, the ducking-stool, debtor's prison, and so on. This one geezer is a moderate case, though, presumably some kind of intellectual. He reads something out to his friend: "The prisoner, with fifteen previous convictions, who feels discriminated against because of his tattoos, is being given laser treatment costing seven thousand marks. Sports projects, to which prisoners are sometimes invited because they have proved socially adaptable, include skiing and canoeing trips lasting several days. The fourteen-year-old, who has a history of one hundred and seventy crimes, is being sent on an adventure holiday to Latin America, costing seventy-three thousand marks. Others are off on a sailing tour costing sixty thousand marks per person."

The short one asks the tall one, "So? Who wrote that?"

The tall one answers, "Somebody called Enzensberger."

The short one says he's right; when he hears something like that, it would make anyone who's led a decent life feel like an idiot.

And the two old men agree with each other's opinions, even with a touch of irony, when one of them says, "Honesty will get you nowhere." It's the title of a book by a man on television who has recently attracted attention because he got a hundred thousand marks for appearing in a three-minute publicity video—incidentally, for the bank where I work.

The short one and the tall one talk about it. The short one says, "Well, if he's got the chance he should take it."

I'm glad he's said that. When all's said and done they think everyone should take his chances wherever he can.

Out of the train, up the escalators. In the subway and particularly on the pavements—mornings more than evenings—in spite of all the greasy ugliness, there's an atmosphere of latent sexuality. The memory of the night before is still fresh in people's minds, and all the other bodies are being examined for their susceptibility to seduction. The bodies still haven't figured that they're on the way to work, and that sexual partnering is irrelevant now. Suddenly, in front of me, there are the two old men again. The tall one says, "I haven't been up this early for ages. You'd almost think we had something to do!" The short one laughs. I push my way between them, try to mutter an "Excuse me!" between my teeth, but I don't manage it, and instead all that comes out is an inarticulate grunting sound that makes them instinctively step aside.

3

The bank district. Grand nineteenth-century palaces stand next to futuristic towers of gleaming steel and black mirrored glass, surrounding a little rectangular, very well-tended French park, where junkies cook up their morning fixes under the bushes. I know a lot of cities, and in nearly all of them the bank district is also the drug district.

Is there a reason for that? Rumenich says the junkies want to be close to where the money is. Office workers on their way in are unsettled by the sight of bloody needles in the gutter—and even more so by meeting the people who have been using them. Sometimes they're just lying around on the footpath, so you have to step over them. These junkies look at you with an animal gaze, brilliant, unnaturally dilated pupils. The police can't get a handle on the situation. From time to time our company brings in a private security service—black-uniformed mercenaries with martial arts training and the task of keeping the front of the building clean and tidy. Then the junkies cluster on the edge of the park. Now and again one of them goes off in search of handouts. "Scusemesirreallysorrytaborryou—jussafewpfennigs—fasomingtoeatstraightupsirscuseme." The completely vain effort of getting the etiquette right! You come here to get on with your business, and you're forever being confronted by these ailing creatures who have lost all dignity. No one wishes them any harm, but there's nothing to be done for them. Meeting them is nothing more than a superfluous embarrassment that you could gladly have done without. They're fucked, anyway. Of course the means are there to clean the place up once and for all, you know that as well as I do, but for some reason the time has never seemed right.

The foyer is a remarkably tasteful ensemble of Carrara marble, chrome, travertine, mirrors, glass facades, and tropical hydroculture that gives me my first high of the morning. That pristine little bell that announces the arrival of the elevator. I walk into its mirrored interior and am confronted by three views of a young businessman on his way to the office: adroit, resolute, optimistic. The faint brownish tint of the mirror gives my skin an even healthier complexion, making me look even younger, fresher, and more successful then I do already. The bank does everything to ensure that its workers feel good. And in turn it demands a lot from them.

Out the elevator and along the corridor with its real Mondrians, Kandinskys, and Mirós to my office. My secretary, Madame Farouche, a Frenchwoman, comes over with a latte macchiato on a silver tray.

No calls until ten, please. I switch on my computer. I play a game. Please enter your surname. Please enter your forename. Please wait a moment. Linda Sonntag will attend to you shortly.

First: Have you graduated from high school?

Yes.

Have you graduated from a university?

Yes.

Do you have a degree in business, marketing, or computing?

Yes.

What do you consider success? Is it your job, the money you earn, or your power over others?

A bit of everything.

Do you consider yourself extremely ambitious? Answer only yes or no.

Yes.

If you could choose, would you opt a) for a badly paid job with good chances of promotion or b) a well-paid job with poor chances of promotion? Choose only a) or b).

a).

In our company we expect an extraordinary amount from our employees. Would you be prepared to work overtime on weekends without additional remuneration?

Yes.

Thank you. You will receive an email from us shortly.

The game is called "Virtual Corporation. Pitiless Competition for the Top Job"! In the foreword to the booklet it says, "Microforum would like to take the opportunity of thanking you for buying 'Virtual Corporation.' You are sure to enjoy playing this game and moving through the intrigues and adventures that form the daily routine in even the world's great corporations. In particular, the many realistic dialogues of this not-too-distant future are sure to remind you of your own personal experiences—and they might even, here and there, correspond to the realities of contemporary business life. The goal of the game is to assume the presidency of Pogodyne Systems. But never forget—it's just a game!"

Do you think it's odd that managerial workers in a bank play computer games in the workplace? This game was installed on every PC on the instructions of company management. Employees are supposed to play it to reinforce their assertiveness skills. To ensure that they also do real work, the game is programmed to switch itself off after a quarter of an hour.

I play one level every morning and increase my virtual fortune. Then, highly motivated, I start work.

4

Ten o'clock. Madame Farouche comes in with the first mail delivery. She is a cultured but not especially intelligent woman. She came to Germany decades ago with her husband, who works as an engineer with an aerospace company. She speaks our language perfectly, and only if you listened very carefully would you discern an accent, which could equally be a suppressed hint of dialect coloring her otherwise perfect German. When I say that she is not especially intelligent, I don't mean that in an insulting way. But she has been working in this department for over ten years and has still not come to terms with certain things that never change. She comes in with the correspondence file and pulls an anxious face. She simply cannot get used to reading letters from people who are going under. I try to cheer her up and say jokingly, as I accept the file, "You know: whoever needs help doesn't deserve it." She gives a pained smile, shrugs her shoulders, and leaves. She doesn't make jokes.

I get letters from people who are going bankrupt every day. Probably hundreds every month. I admit, I was greatly affected by it at first. It sometimes even made me feel quite miserable. But that passed with time. I wouldn't claim to be callous. That's not it. But I've understood that in the field I work in, no one gets poor by accident. That makes many things easier. Indeed, I mean quite seriously what I said to Madame Farouche: Whoever needs help doesn't deserve it.

As I said, I'm deputy manager of the department of foreclosure and liquidation. Bankers are careful to use moderate language. Foreclosure and liquidation, that means: chaos, nervous breakdown, asylum, suicide, murder. Bankers say: We are in a pleasant business relationship with the customer. That means he pays his credit installments on time. They say, A credit is ailing. Which means: The installments are being paid irregularly or not at all. Of course it isn't the credit that is ailing or the bank; the only one who's ailing is the debtor who can't pay, but that is, however understanding one might be of his situation—let's get this straight—*his* damned problem. If a credit has been ailing for long enough, bankers say, The arrangement is no longer tenable. It is at this point that we, the people from the department of foreclosure and liquidation, come on to the scene. We send the customer what is called a final demand. This means: the credit is stopped instantly and immediate repayment of the whole sum is required. By the time the customer receives this letter, he will be finding the business arrangement extremely disagreeable. He calls us to tell us. We say, Sorry to tell you, but the disappointment is all ours. He says, How am I, within fourteen days (let's call it a period of fourteen days' notice for reasons of courtesy), how am I to get hold of (and they're all very different in credit terms) one hundred, one hundred and fifty, eight hundred thousand, or twelve million marks? Unfortunately, we say, we don't know either. But of course we've taken precautions. When the customer still believed his business was going to be a success, all he could see was the money that we had, the money he needed. Of course we'll give it to you, we said, you just have to sign here, here, and here. The mortgage on your house, transfer of all securities, if your wife would please sign this guarantee, thank you very much. In response to this claim, the debtor submits to the immediate appropriation of all his private fortune. People think we write things like that in our contracts to make ourselves feel important, or perhaps as a joke. They're wrong. But they don't believe it. Or else they don't understand it. But it doesn't matter, it all ends up the same. We liquidate. In plain language: We impound everything you have, out from under your ass, every last thing. In certain areas our language is precisely distinguished from that of the bankers. If a credit specialist tells his customer, If things go on like this I'm going to be forced to put our arrangement into liquidation, that means, You are a dead man. The matter is finished, as far as the deal-makers in our company are concerned, and it's our turn. We aren't really bankers, we are the grave diggers in this financial area. We have to make the best of other people's deaths.

If I think about it in those terms, I find my job really terrific. It's like a sport—I squeeze the last drop of blood out of people, and when no one believes there's any left, I give him a good shake, and lo and behold, there's a couple more drops. Of course blood is just a metaphor for money here—and money for blood. Perhaps I should hang it up as a motto in my office: BLOOD FOR MONEY, MONEY FOR BLOOD. But I'm not sure that many people would share my sense of humor. And I'm not entirely sure about metaphor in general, because, as I've said, foreclosure and liquidation means: chaos, nervous breakdown, asylum, suicide, murder. In other words: *real* blood.

So, the mail, what have we got today? Here, for example, is a letter from what we call a small customer with a five-thousand-mark credit. Why has that landed on my desk? Madame Farouche has been playing Mother Teresa again. The man who sent it has probably phoned her up and begged her to give me his earth-shaking letter. I'll have to have a word with her. You want to know what's in the letter? Well, the usual: unemployed for fourteen months . . . wife wants a divorce, children are in counseling . . . attempts to stand on his own two feet have failed . . . mother has cancer . . . faced with financial ruin . . . and so on and so on. I don't want to know any of it, because the fact, reading his file, is this: the man took out a credit of over five thousand to buy himself a wall unit with television for his living room! I wonder how he could have done that, when he knew that the company he worked for was about to go bankrupt. It had been in all the papers. If only he had read the business section rather than the sports pages! On his wages, even the installments must have stretched him. And now my question to you, quite honestly: What does someone who lives in a two-room apartment with his wife and two children, making a worse than pitiful income, need with a wall unit with television? And if he really needs it, why can't he save up, like anyone else? Why does he have to go to the bank and borrow five thousand marks which he will probably never be able to pay back? To be perfectly frank, I'm really not interested in the answer. I couldn't care less. The bank lent the man five thousand and now it wants it back—including interest, of course. And I'm the one who makes sure it gets it. Simple as that. And now I am going to call in good old Madame Farouche and ask her for the thousandth time what's up. Lending money—getting money back with interest; that's a bank's job. And our department's task is to make sure that people pay up.

5

I would be lying if I claimed there was no tension between myself and Rumenich. And I would also be lying if I claimed it didn't matter to me that Rumenich is a woman. And what a woman. The senior level at the bank is occupied mostly by reactionary traditionalists who are extremely reluctant to give managerial positions to women, even if these traditionalists miss no opportunity to stress the opposite as dramatically as possible. Women who want to get ahead in spite of this attitude must therefore be considerably more aggressive than their male colleagues. When Rumenich took over the department of foreclosure and liquidation six months ago, I was warned.

She is extraordinarily attractive and has a very elegant but sharp-featured face that radiates a certain feminine hardness, if I can put it that way. She laughs a lot. The little wrinkles at the corners of her eyes tell you that. Her laughter begins at the top of the scale and has a quite uninhibited ring to it, then it grows darker and develops an edge, and finally it's aimed at whoever she's talking to like the point of a stiletto.

She spent most of her first six months ridding the department of people whose presence she considered inefficient. She explains many of her decisions by saying that this or that is "efficient" or "inefficient." She's left me in peace so far. Once, toward the start, she praised me to other colleagues, saying I could go on working as before. A few weeks later she said—again to colleagues—that she expected more independent thought, particularly from the men in the second level of management, and she looked at me. Since then I've been certain that she's got me in her sights. She isn't attacking, she's just stalking. That irritates me, because I *feel* I'm being watched. I think too much about possible mistakes that I might make, and I immediately make them. She notices and says nothing. Presumably she's taking notes, which she will confront me with when the time is right. I've often wondered whether she's going to discuss them openly with me. But if she really does plan to shoot me down, she could at least let me know. I don't hold that against her. She's tormenting me a bit, but so skillfully that I can't prove anything. For that reason I immediately became disagreeably nervous when she talked to me about the Kosiek case. I try to be worried as little as possible by the atmosphere, by anything ill defined. After all, what's happened so far?

Finally I get her call. Of course she couldn't just pick up the phone and dial my number herself. Her secretary called my secretary and told her Rumenich wanted to talk to me, and then my secretary connected me to *her* secretary, who told me in a condescending tone, "Just a moment. Frau Rumenich wants to talk to you," putting me on hold. For several minutes I listen to an appalling version of Vivaldi's *Four Seasons*, until she answers, with a curt and rising "Yes!," as though I had just pulled her away from her work, which is far more important than any concern of mine could be.

"Thomas Schwarz here. You called me . . ."

"Oh yes, about the Kosiek case . . ."

"Yes . . . ?"

"Don't you think it's time to talk about it? You must be worried about it. It's your area of responsibility, after all."

That's not how I see it, but I don't contradict her. I don't want to annoy her. I say, "Yes, of course."

She gives me a time to come to her office "with my documents."

What's the Kosiek case all about? Good question. No one can really answer that one. I turn up on time for the meeting.

"It's a very complex matter," Rumenich says, offering me a chair that's a foot lower than hers. I stretch my chin over the edge of her desk, like a child.

"Don't you think this is ridiculous?" I ask.

"The Kosiek case?" she asks, arching her eyebrows.

"The chair."

"No, but under the seat to the right you'll find a lever, with which you can operate the hydraulics, if that's what you'd like to do," she says in a completely neutral tone, to make me aware that she would think it utterly ridiculous to interpret the situation in any symbolic way.

Accompanied by a faint hiss from the chair, I rise about nine inches.

"Can we start?"

Rumenich points to a stack of files beside her.

"It's all Kosiek."

I know that. I also know that this stack represents a mere fraction of all the Kosiek files. I answer: "Mmm."

Rumenich starts in on me: "Herr *Schwarz*, you are *dealing* with the matter. What do *you* think of it?"

She's taking no prisoners. The Kosiek portfolio has a few facets too many to be summed up in a few sentences—and Rumenich knows that only too well. And anyway, everyone in our department is responsible for the Kosiek case in some way or another. It existed when I started here four years ago, and even older colleagues who have been here for ten or even twenty years can't remember how it began. Even they were familiar only with parts of it. None of them really has the whole picture, certainly not Rumenich, who sometimes panics, as she might do again today, and then wants someone to come and resolve the whole affair with a single brilliant flourish.

But sadly, there isn't going to be a brilliant flourish, everything's far too complicated for that. As far as I can make out, Kosiek was a construction giant who built up an empire consisting of countless companies with countless buildings, entirely with capital from our bank. The volume of the whole enterprise came to over a billion marks. At some point, in a time of high interest, his capital resources, already pretty thin, ran out, and the bank stopped playing. It got out. It filed claims for compulsory auctions, bankruptcy, compulsory settlements. Some proceedings have been going on for more than twenty years. No one knows how much money the bank has lost in the whole business. Now, if we imagine the worst-case scenario, even the loss of a billion wouldn't really be that significant, as far as the bank was concerned. The unclaimable credits are already written off as tax losses. But of course that isn't an argument that anyone could seriously put forward. Defeatists aren't going to get anywhere in a bank. It's all about saving whatever can be saved. Also, any employee with his sights set on being a manager will get brownie points for carrying out meaningless tasks. If you think I'm being ironic, you're wrong. It's possible—even probable—that an employee who's concerned with the Kosiek case and makes a mistake will suddenly be told that he bears sole responsibility for the missing billion. And you can imagine what happens then—or perhaps you can't.

Young employees hear about the Kosiek case and are immediately keen to go for it because they think they can raise their profile. But they soon realize that it isn't a sure way of currying favor. Rumenich also wants to make her name. Within a year she wants to rid herself of what her predecessor dumped on her fifteen years ago, because she wants to be popular with the board of directors. But everyone in the department knows that fiddling with the Kosiek case brings you nothing but bad luck. They say shit doesn't smell unless you prod it. And they're right.

"We've both wasted a lot of our time here."

I try a friendly smile, but she isn't buying.

"Quite honestly, I can't see that I have the sole responsibility . . ."

Rumenich gives me a penetrating look and says nothing. I manage to hold her gaze for a while, before I turn my eyes to the floor. She waits for me to do that, and only then does she continue.

"I'm relying on you, Herr Schwarz."

I feel miserable on the way back to my desk. Why me, of all people? I wonder. The answers I find are anything but comforting. Do I have to save my job now? This year I was hoping to become head of the department of foreclosure and liquidation. Then they dumped Rumenich on me. Originally it was supposed to be for only three months. That time ran out ages ago, and they've stopped talking about interim solutions. Of course no one's told me I'm to be promoted. But if you're the deputy head of department, it's only logical that at some point you're going to be head of department, isn't it? I urgently have to see what I can do in the Kosiek case.

6

Marianne's aunt is coming to stay for the weekend, and after an argument that lasted several days, I've already agreed to be available on Saturdays and Sundays, at least in the afternoon. In fact there's nothing wrong with Marianne's aunt, but I don't get on terribly well with elderly people. It has nothing to do with age as such, just the particular *generation* she belongs to. She's arriving on the train. I'm waiting for her at the platform. Marianne's at home clearing up the apartment, getting a welcome cocktail ready. I can't see why Marianne's going to quite so much trouble. She, on the other hand, says she just wants to "make things nice" for when her aunt comes. And the one thing I really can't bear is that particular kind of "niceness."

I spot Olivia the minute she gets off the train. We greet each other with a warm hug and I take her luggage from her. On the way to the parking lot she tells me about her husband, who is currently giving the opening speech at a conference in Bolivia. He's a professor of oral surgery.

We reach our car—Marianne and I drive a small Japanese car, a Subaru, cheap, not expensive to run, and perfectly adequate for the city. But it's embarrassing to me now; Olivia's suitcase only just fits in the trunk. She herself clambers with noticeable difficulty into the passenger seat. She would never say anything, not even in jest, she's too tactful for that. I wonder: Why don't we drive a Mercedes, which we could actually afford? We were going to wait until I was promoted, when I would get a company BMW. But that's only part of the truth. We're worried about paying so much for a car. Why is that, actually? Because I've always had a nagging suspicion that our relative affluence was something very temporary.

As far as Olivia's concerned, the little car is "charming," I think, or at least she's trying to see things that way, that much I'm sure of.

She briefly asks how we are. I give a generic reply—that is, I say, "Fine, thanks!" and then she immediately starts talking again, while I drive her through the streets in more or less complete silence.

Her husband, the oral surgeon, has developed a new kind of operation that means that the shattered jaws of accident victims can be more or less reconstructed. At the moment he's traveling around the world to present his work at specialist conferences and bring it to a wider audience. Olivia has gone with him to Amsterdam, New York, and Cairo, but now she's decided to spend summer at home. Her husband comes home at least every other week, bringing with him exciting stories and presents from distant lands. Then they invite their friends—professors, writers, intellectuals, industrialists, and God knows who else—to nice little parties.

Olivia likes to talk about the modest beginnings of their life together, back in the sixties. The one-and-a-half-room apartment where they lived after their first baby was born, the toilet on the landing, the meager income of her young husband, who had just graduated and was working as an assistant, and who was already demonstrating the promise of brilliant scientific talents. Then, later, the first professional successes, the first real money, soon after that the first house, four children, all of whom, of course, had done brilliantly. Ah yes, the children. Their musical talents were nurtured with such devoted attention. They all learned instruments. Sextets were performed at family parties, almost up to professional standard. Nowadays, with the children all out of the house, less music is played, but when the family comes together, there are always lots of these friends whose lives have been no less fortunate. I have been present at several such occasions. There's a cheerful, cosmopolitan, somewhat intellectual atmosphere. You're forever catching scraps of sentences like "Oh yes, and then he actually got the Yale professorship," "To judge by your most recent publications, you and I see pretty much eye to eye," "Our youngest is about to be selected for the regional football team. But with his mathematical abilities—he's been the best in his class for years—we hope, of course, that he won't give it all up just for sport," and so on and so on.

I sit in the corner, green with envy, and feel what a pleb I am. Whenever anyone asks me what I do, I'm ashamed to tell them. A dumbfounded philosophy professor to whom I explained what my work consisted of, said to himself, almost in a whisper, "Ah, that's not so good."

There's no point mentioning that none of these people have even the slightest financial worries, apart from investments and taxes, of course. On more than one occasion I've heard people say, regarding my job, "Of course, someone has to do it."

It wouldn't be that much different if I said I was in charge of a prison. They would still be in complete agreement that "someone" had to do that as well, but at the same time they would see me as a kind of criminal because I spent all day in jail.

But what's much more crucial is that there isn't anything intellectual about my job, nothing that serves the good of mankind, nothing that makes the world a better place. Fixing shattered jaws— now there's a point to that! As indeed there is to artistic and social professions of any kind. On the other hand, raking in cash for a bank—that's the pits.

Things aren't much better for Marianne. As an advertising executive she's "creative," but only where money's concerned, where industry's concerned, nothing more elevated than that.

The real puzzle for me is how the generation of Aunt Olivia and her husband have managed to earn a huge amount of money in absolutely secure jobs, and to see that as the most natural thing in the world. I've never heard these people utter a single word of doubt—of doubt about themselves, I mean—or any reference to their unabashed good fortune. They simply hold the opinion that this wealth is naturally their due, that it's obtainable because of their outstanding abilities, and that for that reason they have quite naturally and literally earned it.

No one has ever earned anything; they've just gotten ahold of it. I've seen some of *their* people going under as well—although not that many of them. And there was nothing they could do.

In her smart summer dress—it's modern and yet it suits her as a sixty-year-old—Olivia moves with that same confidence, clearly to be distinguished from self-aggrandizement and yet capable of arousing envy. We stand on the balcony of our apartment and talk about the area. I point to the shops in the row opposite and deliver my prognoses about which one will go bankrupt when. She says she feels sorry for these people. That's nice of her, but it's just as meaningless if she had said she didn't, although of course it sounds better.

We have an excellent dinner, the three of us, cooked by Marianne. Three courses, with delicious French red wine. Olivia has brought a classical CD that was recommended in *Die Zeit*, which creates a stylish atmosphere. Marianne has put out a candelabra that we normally never use, and for two or three hours I manage to feel a part of this perfectly functioning, wonderfully harmonious and imaginative world, the world of Olivia, who is so generous as to allow us to share in her joie de vivre. Thank you, Olivia, thank you!

When I lie down in bed, drunk from the heavy red wine, I think of Rumenich again, the Kosiek case, which I'd managed to forget about for the evening. My life strikes me as petty, I feel petty myself, I'd love to be a professor of something or other, giving important lectures at far-off universities. I hope Olivia doesn't come and see us again too soon.

7

ast year the building and loan section of our bank gave me the book *It's a Lovely Day Today* as a Christmas present. Every building-and-loan customer with savings of more than fifty thousand gets a copy. It has a saying for every day of the year. They're simple, and tend to insult the reader's intelligence. I read them if I'm not feeling so great. One of them says, "You're an extraordinary person, and you know that today will be a successful one for you. Look forward to it." I wonder to myself: Are *all* savers with a sum of over fifty thousand in the bank extraordinary people? What a breathtaking idea—thousands upon thousands of building-and-loan savers sitting in their beds in the evening, reading aloud to themselves, "You're an extraordinary person . . ."

Are you extraordinary? Does the very fact that everyone is, in a literal sense, extraordinary, not make us all irrevocably ordinary?

I admit it's pure masochism that sends me back to this idiotic book, time and again. I figure it's good common sense for my employer to keep me supplied with this kind of edifying reading matter. Everything about it is fantastic. The fact that it's so thin, that many of my colleagues have it as well, and read it, that it's so positive— "You're hoping for a new job? Go to the one you've got with fresh enthusiasm, and it will seem as good as new!"—that it really explains the whole world—the *whole* world—with a single instruction: Think positive! I love this book because its sole purpose is to free me from the burden of individuality, I can feel that very clearly. I go to the bank, I work industriously, and if I do it properly, my life will be happy. At first Marianne used to laugh at me when she caught me with this book, but these days I keep finding it on her bedside table, more and more often. Clearly she can't resist its charms, either.

I can sense that our marriage is under threat, but I can't work out why. It would make perfect sense if my book had a perfect, pat solution for that, too. It says: "The victor sees defeats and problems as a challenge. Start enjoying failure, too."

I'll have to get on with my work for now.

A meeting in the bank's conference room with Rumenich, Bellmann, and a few others. Our client Findeisen is there, too. A disaster waiting to happen. How did the bank manage to ignore the fact for five years? This guy has debts upon debts, and there he sits in the most expensive outfits, with a lime-green cell phone in his top pocket and a red Ferrari outside the front door. The credit specialists in particular hate him for the Ferrari. Rumenich launches in on the conversation without preliminaries, with a straight blow to the chin: "We've been keeping an eye on you for a long time, Herr Findeisen, a long time. And now we've had enough."

Findeisen has drops of sweat on his brow. Of course he knows we weren't calling him in for a cup of coffee. But he hopes he can get us to postpone things one more time. It's always worked before.

"At least let me have the four hundred thousand. Just until next month, then I can pay the laborers and get on with the next phase of building."

Rumenich says coldly, "No more subs, no more time. That's it. You should have been finished long ago with the time you've had already. Where is our *money*?"

Findeisen has invested in "the East," and lost a pile of money. He used to show me all kinds of plans. In one area somewhere to the east of Berlin, a "greenfield site," as he had always proudly asserted, there was to be a magnificent estate of fourteen identical eight-story blocks, a "supermarket mall," and various other eyesores whose purpose I could only vaguely understand. I didn't know the background of this project. I just knew that Findeisen's bubble had burst and every single mark that he had sunk into the business was gone. Findeisen saw this as ingratitude on the part of "those fucking

Easterners," as he put it, because whenever he talked about East Germans he always called them, every single time, "those fucking Easterners." They weren't interested in his buildings, in fact they had organized a grassroots campaign against their construction. They didn't want any new prefabs, they said. The people at the bank who had helped to support this dubious plan are now annoyed, too, of course, so they want to see Findeisen hang.

It really isn't easy for characters like Findeisen. No one likes them. But now, as he sits there, pleading with Rumenich, sweating more and more disagreeably and probably about to disintegrate into his various component parts, I could almost feel sorry for him. Hard as it is to believe, he's wearing flesh-colored silk socks with chestnut-brown slippers. The veins in Findeisen's temples are swelling, fat as twigs. His head has turned maroon. For a moment it looks as though he might die on the spot, but then he doesn't. Five or six times he pleads with Rumenich, as a dog pleads with his mistress, but the mistress says with a smile, "*Rien ne va plus.*" Findeisen leaves. The odds of him killing himself are pretty damned good.

On the way back to our offices, Bellmann claps me good-naturedly on the shoulder and says, "The victor sees defeats and problems as a challenge. Start enjoying failure, too." I give a startled laugh, and quietly regret the fact that in the field of reading, I'm clearly not an inch ahead of Bellmann.

8

Olivia's visit made me think, as her visits always do. I think about my life and, to comfort myself, take my job application documents out of my desk drawer in my office. Look, everything's exactly as it should be! First-class references! Recommendations and assessments that you can see and touch! All of these pieces of paper, stamped and signed, portray me as a great white hope, someone who's been invested in, someone on whom society has staked a great deal. Really, anyone reading it would have to admit that my life has run along orderly lines—and more than that, I've achieved something in my thirty-five years.

What I have lying in front of me—my résumé, my "curriculum vitae"—describes a laudable adaptability, an intelligence slightly above the average, and the very mixture of thoughtfulness and hard work that such a document is supposed to represent. They talk about "white spaces" on CVs—it would be more appropriate, in this context, to talk about "black holes," but in the euphemistic diction of the world of work, they only ever talk about "white spaces." In my CV, there aren't any.

I was born, there's no possible doubt about that, I went to schools and a university and got good marks on my exams, I took practical tests and did my military service as one is supposed to do. Everywhere I have been, I've been awarded papers that attest to my regular attendance and my achievements, which go beyond the average requirements.

Blameless, you'd think. Admittedly, there's the occasional blemish—my studies, which, on closer examination, took longer than they should have, a period of more than fifteen years at school—but nothing intolerable, as any recruitment officer would agree.

Of course these documents reveal nothing of my anxiety, my anger, my despair, my love, my happiness, my unhappiness. Then again, I presume that they don't need to, because none of it is of any real significance as long as it doesn't make you stand out from the crowd, as long as you don't start falling out of the frame.

However, some people with presentable CVs like mine are locked up in institutions and suffer from anxiety or obsessive-compulsive disorders. Others shoot themselves in front of the TV cameras on the roof of—let's say—a bank that they've just robbed while wearing a stocking mask over their heads. Still others quietly succumb to alcohol or get involved in infernal divorce wars, or both; and some of them, armed to the teeth, storm a branch of McDonald's on the instructions of some extraterrestrial power and exterminate umpteen people who die while chewing on cheeseburgers—and so on.

But the overwhelming majority of people with presentable CVs like mine celebrate fiftieth anniversaries at work, receive loyalty bonuses from their employers, retire at the expected time, and have their death notice in the paper paid for by the company.

I can't say with any certainty which group I will belong to in the end. The way things look at the moment, the second is more likely, the people with the golden anniversary and the death notice. But who knows whether one day I might not surprise Rumenich with a hand grenade under her table?

What do you reveal, oh CV of mine, in the way of drunken parties—and I've been to plenty of those—of nights of ecstasy with women I'd never set eyes on before and whose names I never knew—or did know but have forgotten long ago? Do you have anything to say about the blackness in my brain, about my darkest curses, my secret laughter? Do you mention the fact that I've considered murder? Do you say, to give just one example, where it indicates "married," that after Olivia left, Marianne threw a half-full cup of coffee at me, which shot past my ear and exploded against the wall? The sight of the crater it left in the plaster made me angrier than the fact that it had been thrown. I'd have been killed if she'd hit me. And at the same place—"married"—do you mention the fact that I tried, vodka bottle in one hand and claw hammer in the other, to knock the lock out of the bedroom door when Marianne had locked herself in? Do you mention that while I was doing this, I emitted noises like a furious ape-man? You see, you don't mention any of that.

And neither, oh CV, do you mention that when I was writing you down, I felt like a con artist, a polished one admittedly, but still a con artist, a fraudster, because I've managed to pepper my lies so perfectly with little truths that no one can tell the two apart. But that's not fair, you reply; you have to learn to distinguish between private and professional life, because any human being lives two lives. And as long as the barbarian you are in your private life doesn't find his way into the office of his perfectly behaved doppelgänger, everything is fine. That's well attested.

I ask myself whether I should send a bunch of flowers to Marianne's workplace, but then I decide to leave it. It would just be tasteless.

9

fetch Bellmann from his office, to go and have lunch with him in the cafeteria. I walk in and open the door without knocking. He's on the phone. He waves me in and points at the seat opposite. I sit down and he switches his phone to speaker. He grins at me and bites the tip of his tongue. A pleading woman's voice, telling the usual story that clearly amuses Bellmann, although he's heard it several thousand times in several thousand variations: the minute her husband opened the letter from the bank, he had collapsed in the hall. It was his heart. He had worked day and night for the company, he had done everything humanly possible. That letter had been the final blow from which he would never recover if things were left as they were. They had counted every single penny, but they never made much of a profit outside of the season. They really didn't know where to go from here, et cetera, et cetera. Bellmann listens to this for a while and makes a pinched face. Then he puts her off—he doesn't have the file in front of him right now, he'll take another look, he wishes her husband a swift recovery, he'll see whether anything can be done. The woman goes on talking. Bellmann hangs up, stands, grabs his jacket, and asks what's on the menu.

Lunchtime conversations with colleagues revolve around practical matters. They like to describe their own journeys on public transportation from home to the office. They talk about where and how often they have to change and the fact that they reach their place of work in an astonishingly short time, generally. They talk about special holiday offers and compare Continental winter tires with Universal winter tires. Every now and then, all of a sudden and without warning, one of them will insert a small and dirty joke into the conversation. That tends to happen when someone has noticed that a word that had just been used has an obscene double meaning. Like "insert," heh-heh-heh. Now and then one of them will pull out a trump card and talk about a book that he's read. Bellmann loves Italy and talks a lot about cooking. Or about government foreign policy. Colleagues like to discuss political subjects in general. Each person who speaks tries to find a particularly polished turn of phrase as though he were a government spokesman, or whatever. After lunch you spend a little time complaining to your most intimate colleague about how self-important everyone is.

My most intimate colleague is Bellmann. We take our pear *Belle Hélène* into his office because we've got other things to discuss. Bellmann can't be a threat to me because he hasn't the slightest chance of getting an important position. We started at the bank together after we finished our studies. I got promoted, he didn't. Neither of us quite knows why, because he's not bad at his job. Rumenich once confided in me that she thought Bellmann lacked that "certain something." Her predecessor must have seen things similarly, and recent of course I haven't contradicted her. I tell Bellmann about my recent conversation with Rumenich. He listens thoughtfully, then he says, "You're going to have to be careful."

I ask him to get ahold of any available files on the Kosiek case and to make a list of the files in circulation. I explain that I plan to produce a watertight account of the whole business, which will protect me if Rumenich ever hits on the idea of firing me. Bellmann promises to help.

It's time to get on with the day's business.

I have to get to a meeting. The taxi that Madame Farouche calls for me is a disaster. Inside it stinks like an ashtray, and hanging from the rearview mirror there's a little smelly tree marked NEW CAR FRAGRANCE. It's completely useless, of course. I get into the backseat and, a bit tight-lipped, just give the address. I don't feel like engaging in the kind of chat you usually get in taxis, but I can *sense* that the taxi driver wants a conversation. He seems preoccupied with my business suit and the fact that I'm coming out of a bank.

"Lots of meetings, I bet?" he begins vaguely.

"Of course," I answer coolly. It occurs to me that I've been a bit too dismissive and I add, "You must have commitments of your own." Without being aware of it I have just provided the keyword to the speech he probably delivers to all his passengers: *commitments*. Oh yes, he's got plenty of those, or, to put it a bit less elegantly: his debts are slowly but surely killing him.

"As you may be able to tell from my voice, I haven't always been a taxi driver. I'm a doctor. For years I was an editor with a specialist medical press. At some point the owner lost interest, liquidated the business, and retired to Switzerland. I've seen photographs of this elegant gentleman's villa. I'd very much like to go there. But there's no point. The bastard. Then I went freelance and was broke after two years. Since then I've been a taxi driver. Now you know."

"And I don't give a shit!" I'm about to say, but I hold myself back. What should I say? He's bothering me with his private affairs. All you can say in response to something like that is: too bad, bad luck. He wants pity, he wants to hear something like: It can happen to anyone. But people who live the way I do—with a job and money and so on—don't think that way. They think: It's your own fault. Except, if the same thing happens to them, they think: How unjust, but it can happen to anyone. This man must be aware of that; he's been on the other side, after all. I think he's letting things slide. But when I get out, I give him a one-mark tip.

Outside the Gothic Palace I meet Heinz Schmidt, a particularly scruffy bailiff who smells faintly of spirits, as he always does.

I say, "I'll do the talking."

He nods. I need him only to make this business official. Then we go inside.

I've never seen anything like the Gothic Palace before. I assume very few people have. Outside the entrance there hangs an enormous hardboard sign with a painting of a knights' castle under a stormy sky, presumably done by the owner, whose artistic talent is more or less that of a moderately gifted thirteen-year-old. What prompted the bank to give this place credit? The truth is, the official in charge of the case didn't understand what the "Gothic Palace" was supposed to be. He might have been expecting a shop selling devotional objects. And in any case the security was sound. And now we find out the truth—the owner is a tubby, heavy-metal type who pretends to be a Satanist but really isn't. And that thing beside him is presumably what he calls his "fiancée." They sell comic figures, comics, death-metal records and CDs, horror videos, and computer games—trash, pure trash. Expensive trash that nobody wants. So of course they've gone broke.

My aggression in this case is directed toward their idiotic, infantile lack of worldliness. As if there weren't enough problems in the world already, these half-wits invent a few more. I mean, what sort of an attitude is that, wanting to spend your whole life playing at being a knight and fighting plastic dragons and monsters? I'm going to have to teach them a bit of reality, with a good hard dose of compulsory repossession.

"I imagine you're going to think me sadistic or fascistic, if you happen to know what that means," I say when we walk in, Schmidt and I. While I'm talking I walk up and down in a leisurely manner, brush a speck off my jacket, glance at my gold watch. I want to provoke the guy, I want him to think I'm one of the monsters he sells in his shop, but in the form of an unscrupulous, early-capitalist parvenu. I run the tips of my fingers across the comic figures on the shelves. A foot and a half tall, each one hand-painted and costing three hundred marks. "Superman, Batman, Catwoman, Robin, the Riddler—impressive, really impressive." I walk over to the video shelf and bump into a big box bearing the inscription *The Blob.*

Inside are about a hundred cassettes of *The Blob.* The heavy-metal guy mutters something about a search warrant.

"Herr Schmidt, show our customer what he wants to see."

Schmidt does so. Then the fiancée starts howling that she's going to call the police, and the heavy-metal guy shouts that he's paid all his debts.

I say, "That's so not true. You're fifty thousand in the red, and you've had three months. That's it now." I pick up a *Blob* cassette, walk over to him, and hold it under his nose. "That—is worthless crap!"

"It's what people want."

"Obviously not that much. Look. How idiotic would somebody have to be to watch a film called *The Blob?* You see, you're costing my company money. Money for which serious men and women have done good, hard work. And you borrow that money and buy yourself a box full of *Blob* because you think that's a business plan. But it isn't a business plan, I swear to you, it's utterly *pathetic!*"

The rest is routine. I get Schmidt to stick his seal all over the place. There's the usual howling and moaning. "No, not that, not that!" and so on—and then we go.

I say, "The stuff'll be picked up tomorrow. And if there's anything missing, we'll have the lawyers on to you. Goodbye."

Strangely, at that moment I think about that thing we say to children: "If you take this or that away from your friend, he'll be very sad." But in fact people aren't sad at all if you take something away from them. They're furious. The heavy-metal guy's fiancée pulls open the door behind us and shouts, "We'll never give up, bank fucker!" Without turning around, I throw back my head and laugh loudly. Then I say, "Schmidt, you heard: bank fucker. They're just begging me to bring slander charges."

Schmidt nods bluntly. Presumably he's thinking about how much the impounded goods are going to fetch at auction.

10

S unday morning. Marianne's in the kitchen getting something ready for dinner. We have people coming. I'm sitting in the living room, unwashed, in my pajamas and dressing gown, and battling against something that I would call panic attacks if I knew exactly what the phrase meant. Nothing has happened, or at least nothing specific. I have a day off and nothing to do. Maybe that's it. I had to promise Marianne I wouldn't go to the office today. I was there yesterday, and I'd have liked to go in again today. I want to try and describe my anxiety states: they begin around the top of the belly, then they rise to the chest, which expands, and from there they move into the lymph system. Finally, via the lymph canals along the side of the throat, they reach the head, the brain, trickling into it like a searing fluid. I think I'm starting to go mad, but I don't know why. Have I forgotten something? That's what it feels like: as if I'd forgotten something important, something that couldn't be put off. But however much I think about it, I can't imagine what it could be. Of course it has something to do with work. I can see before my eyes the mountains of files that Bellmann has put together for me about the Kosiek case. For days he kept coming into my office, carrying massive stacks of files in front of him, and they were soon piled up three feet high on the floor by my desk. I find it reassuring to be near these files. They are dangerous—no human being alive could remember everything inside them. And their content is far from unambiguous. Many of these documents are amenable to different interpretations, some of the memos are incomplete, others have been deliberately misrepresented. Someone will have dropped one thing under a desk and picked up something else. Different specialists have had different views of how different things were to be done. They assembled notes in which they never directly attacked the position of their predecessor or adversary, but made imperceptible corrections. All of that has to be read, read properly, skillfully interpreted. But I don't know how to do it!

I urgently have to get to the office.

Marianne comes into the room and reproaches me about what I look like, tells me to go to the bathroom and get myself ready and help her in the kitchen. I obey. Her work colleagues are coming this evening. Marianne works in an advertising agency. I don't know her colleagues, but I imagine them as an easygoing and pretty informal crowd. At the moment they're busy with a large-scale campaign for a chain of burger restaurants. It's an important account which, according to Marianne, could save the agency from going bankrupt. Tonight, of course, we're having hamburgers.

We prepare the onion rings, the mince, the sesame buns, the slices of gherkin and tomato, and enjoy our perfect kitchen suite. I try to explain to Marianne that the files have a life of their own. She laughs. I laugh, too. She says it's as though the files wake up like creatures in a fairy tale the minute you leave them unattended. You turn around for a minute and immediately they're plotting behind your back. Marianne runs her hand over my head as if I were a patient giving cause for concern, and says, "Just stay cool, don't start talking nonsense."

It's early afternoon, everything's ready for the evening, the hamburger ingredients are on the plates and in bowls in the fridge. We've put a long table in the sitting room and arranged it and set up the portable electric grill. Marianne has devotedly decorated the table with items from the hamburger campaign that she has brought home from the office. It's all arranged so charmingly that it immediately puts me in a bad mood. And yet once I'm certain that there's absolutely nothing left to do, I give Marianne a pained glance, and I'm suddenly struck by the desire, like a shaft of light through the darkness, to have sex with her. She happens to be standing in the bedroom, anyway. I lean against the door frame with my elbow raised and ask her if she's up for it.

"Sure, fine," she says.

"Sure, fine," I think, as I'm taking off my trousers. What does "Sure, fine" mean? Marital sex on a Sunday afternoon—sure, fine? Couldn't we be a bit more enthusiastic? Or at least a bit less sort of "sure, fine"? I like Marianne's body. I like to smell it, to stroke it, but she isn't moving right. Not that she couldn't if she wanted to, but I know what's wrong—her head's full of hamburger. I ask her if she's thinking about the campaign. I ask sympathetically, understandingly. "Yes," she says, and then we talk about it. Her hopes, her fears, the agency, the money, her colleagues, how everything's going to be, the fact that you can never be sure, and so on and so on. Finally it's time to get dressed, the guests will be here soon. I wonder if I should give myself a hand job while Marianne's in the bath, but that would put an irrevocable seal on the mess we've just made of making love in the afternoon.

In the evening I feel both calm and melancholy, and drink heavy French red wine, which suits me better than the awful American beer the others are knocking back. Werner, Marianne's boss, a guy in his late thirties with collar-length black hair, a tanned complexion, a positive expression—isn't that what they say?—wants to be my friend, at least for this evening. I admire him for his good mood, which seems to be the rule where he's concerned. How can he be in a good mood when he's up to his ears in debt? He flirts jokingly with Marianne, but he's really doing it for my benefit, because he's keeping a close eye on me to make sure I'm catching it all. By ten o'clock he's drunk, but not unpleasantly so. He sits down beside me, puts his arm around my shoulders, and calls me "Tommy."

"Come on, Tommy, can't you get your bank to set aside a few million for us? There'd be a few thousand in it for you, too!"

Yells of laughter from the assembled company. I reply that I'm not one of the bank people responsible for giving out the money; I'm one of the people who take it back. Werner takes his hand off my shoulder. He seems to have sobered up a little. "So what sort of thing do you do there?"

"Foreclosure and liquidation." And I explain it to him, if not in all its astounding details. I don't want to deprive him of his hopes for his business, because it certainly wouldn't do much for Marianne's career. I notice that he's made up his mind not to spoil the good atmosphere. He drinks another beer, has another burger grilled for him, and again and again he clinks glasses with his colleagues and raises toasts to me: "To our host!"

By half past eleven he's plastered, very unpleasantly this time. He takes out his wallet and bangs it on the table. He doesn't want to have any debts in the banker's house. There's too much of a risk that I'll haul him up before the bailiff. At first everybody laughs, then they realize he's serious. They try to calm him down, but they are only partially successful. The atmosphere tips over, it's actually quite embarrassing, and everyone tries, for politeness's sake, to save something that can no longer be saved. Werner is slurring, so soon they'll be able to make a joke out of it. Everybody decides to call it a day. Werner bids Marianne an extravagant farewell. He feints a few boxing moves at me before he starts to sway and stumbles over the shoe closet, falling headlong into the hall. His colleagues help him to his feet, amid pained and embarrassed laughter. Finally they're all out of the house.

We clear up. Marianne fights back tears. I'm boiling with rage because I know she's blaming me, but I say nothing, and afterward we don't say another word about it.

11

f I look at my friend Markus, for example, I feel ill at ease. In his position I'd probably lose it completely, but perhaps when you actually are in difficulties, things don't look quite so desperate. That's always the astonishing thing about compulsory repossessions—the fact that the very people in the most hopeless situations go about with the most extravagant hopes, utterly harebrained.

On the other hand, a few thousand more or less per month, who's that going to bother in the long term? Only somebody without any money at all. Like my friend Markus, for example, who is also one of the bank's clients. Markus writes screenplays, but he's never sold one. I like the things he does. He works as a journalist on the side to make some money, but he hardly earns a thing. My nightmare is that his credit details are going to land here on my desk one day, and that I'm going to have to repossess everything he owns, over some pathetic sum of ten or twenty thousand, it can't be more than that. In fact I do everything I can to make sure it doesn't come to that, and keep lending the idiot money he never pays back—five thousand marks two months ago. And I've never had a single mark back. Nevertheless I've known him for too long. I'd never take any action against him.

Of course the bastard knows that, and grins and says, "Hey, I want to fly to Hong Kong with Petra. She's got cash but I'm completely broke. You know how it is. Five thousand, just till the autumn, okay?" What am I supposed to do? Of course I give him the five thousand. Whatever, I'm supposed to be having lunch with him today, maybe, he wasn't absolutely sure if he had time. He's busy getting divorced. Not from Petra, she's his girlfriend. From Babs, his wife. I can't even think about what's about to hit him—and me. It would make you weep. She's going to take him to the cleaners.

Markus and I have arranged to meet at the Caravaggio, one of the fashionable Italian places here, where businessmen lubricate their negotiations and ladies who can afford it—after they've gone shopping at Prada, Gucci, Helmut Lang, Versace, or wherever—wash down their gamberoni all'aglio, olio, e peperoncino with a glass of Lacryma Christi del Vesuvio bianco, and so on.

By the time I walk in, Markus hasn't turned up. I go to the table where we always sit, a table for two. Our lunches together are a ritual that we keep to at ever greater intervals, and the subjects we talk about are always the broadest imaginable—life in general, you might say. Right now we have to have a lunch because of his divorce from Babs, of course. Last week she came back from a trip with a girlfriend, and he collected her from the station, and not out of attentiveness, as she probably knew all too well. Markus just couldn't bear waiting till they got home—he was in too much of a hurry to tell her he'd been cheating on her.

It wasn't a surprise. Some weeks previously he'd met a woman filmmaker with whom he wanted to make a documentary about something or other. He liked her, I could tell by the way he told me that nothing would ever come of it, not in this life. I was immediately sure that something *would* come of it, but only if he had decided once and for all to end his marriage. Last week, when Babs went on a trip, I didn't hear a word from him for three days, and then I got the phone call. I asked, "What's up?"

"What d'you think."

"Go on, what?"

"Wild nights with Frau Berger."

He'd done it, and because he'd done it, he charged up to his beloved wife at the station to tell her as quickly as possible. And when he told me about it, he kept using phrases like "making a clean break," "dotting the i's," "letting people know what's what," and so on.

Babs didn't react with the scene he had feared. Not at all. Markus was flabbergasted: "It just took a minute. I said I was in love with Petra, and she said, Let's get divorced, then."

But clearly it had gone further than that. That was why we were meeting today. Certainly Babs had spent the next night with *her* lover—whose existence she had always denied until then—and Markus had gone to Petra's, and when the two of them—Markus and Babs—left their shared apartment, they behaved like an old married couple setting off for their day's work: Have you seen my keys? Don't forget your jacket. When will you be home? Kiss? See you.

But something must have gone wrong with Babs's lover, because the next day she called Markus and said, "You're going to wish you'd never been born, you can be sure of that."

The threat had come in the context of the car, a Fiat Panda that belonged to both of them. Markus had said they'd be able to reach some kind of agreement.

"She's going to take *everything* from you. You've humiliated her," I say, when Markus comes in and joins me.

"Yeah, yeah," says Markus.

He absentmindedly runs his finger along the edge of his empty wine glass. He looks very much the worse for wear.

"I need your advice, Thomas. What should I do now?"

He starts talking about himself and Babs. Their sex life has gone all to hell. They'd recently tried to sleep together after hours of fighting. In the old days they'd had their best sex after their most violent rows—and this time he couldn't even get it up. That hadn't been so great. He'd been thinking about Petra. He'd stopped finding Babs's body attractive. Not that it had been the most important thing in their marriage. But he had already started wondering: Is this the way you want to get old? Like *this?*

Things with Petra were quite different. He couldn't believe that something like this had happened to him again. He'd thought that was all in the past. And it had been four years since he'd really been in love.

"Why can't I be happy this time, too?"

I interrupt him with the occasional "mmm," "sure," and "of course," but I don't get what he's talking about. Most crucially, I don't understand what he wants from *me*. Sure I'm his friend, so I'm obliged to listen to this. But what's he trying to tell me? I have difficulty concentrating. Things aren't much better for me and Marianne, after all. And I think it's interesting that Babs didn't make a scene. I'm afraid it would be different with Marianne.

12

There's a party mood in the Schwarz household. Marianne has brought a bottle of Piper Heidsieck (red label) home from work. She's been promoted to "account manager" for the big hamburger offensive. We have a hot bath, drinking champagne, and after that we fuck like the devil.

Marianne tells me, cheeks flushed: Werner, her boss, had called her in and told her it wasn't like him to apologize, but she should know that nothing that had happened would have any effect on her work situation. And then he asked her if she'd take charge of the hamburger campaign.

Marianne had agreed immediately. Such a success! She'd started as an assistant in the agency only a year ago, with responsibility for the coffee machine and the phone, and now she had an account of her own, and such an important one for the company.

I point out that that's odd, since she told me that the agency's survival depends on the success of this commission.

"Odd? What's odd about it?"

Marianne is almost shouting, so I'm immediately aware that I've made another fatal error, and one for which there's no redress. My remark proves that I thought she wasn't up to the task.

"But you are, you are—of course you are!"

"Only a man could do it. A man like you!"

"What's *that* supposed to mean? Nevertheless, your friend Werner behaved like an alcoholic ape at our party! He's handing the account over to you because he knows it's going down the tubes. He wants to get the hell out just in time, and you and your account are going to end up covered in shit."

"You're sick. You're paranoid. I really wonder how you manage to do your work. You're probably feeling guilty because you ruin all those people."

"I don't ruin anybody. The people I take action against were ruined long ago. I have nothing to do with it. I just enforce it. That Werner is an asshole. You saw how he behaved. You're not going to tell me you believe he's loyal to you?"

"I haven't the faintest idea what you're talking about."

Oh my God—why didn't I notice it before?

"You've got a thing going with him, haven't you?"

She looks at me, startled, and doesn't say a word.

"Go on, you're seeing him, that's it. Admit it!"

"You're crazy."

"He spent that whole lovely, long evening coming on to you. I saw it, I'm not blind."

"Just a few days ago you were telling me that it was *you* he was after!"

"That stupid laugh of yours just proves I'm right."

"You're mad, you're bonkers."

She starts crying, jumps up, and holds a sheet in front of her body as though I mustn't see her naked anymore, even though we've just slept together. She dashes to the bathroom and locks herself in.

Oh, how I hate it! I take my copy of *It's a Lovely Day Today* out from under the bed and try to find a suitable passage. "Make a firm decision today, to double the enthusiasm you have put into your life so far."

I have a stirring of regret. I'm sure Werner's going to fire Marianne. At first she'll go to bed with him out of gratitude, if she hasn't done that already, and then she'll fuck up this dumb campaign because she has no chance of *not* fucking it up.

Later Marianne sits slightly drunk on the living room sofa, with her legs drawn up as she clutches her almost empty champagne bottle. I sit at the living room table and go through my bank statements.

"There's nothing going on with Werner."

I wait a while before I say, "Sure, I believe you."

I have serious doubts about whether I can believe her. It's strange, but I've never been bothered by the question of whether Marianne would play around. But the question's there now.

"I'm just concerned about you."

"In the wrong way, though, Tom. In the wrong way."

13

Bellmann comes in and asks if I feel like going to Lehmann's, or more precisely, he pulls the door open and shouts, "That's enough work for today, Schwarz. You've had long enough. Come and have a few pints of Guinness."

I can't really figure out how come he's in such a good mood. Bellmann, who usually creeps so anxiously along the corridor. Has he been promoted? Is he inviting me out for a beer to celebrate the fact that he's just been given my job? I don't think he's as relaxed as he seems. He's more the type to be racked with doubts if something like that had happened. He'd lose weight, he'd stop—rather than start—drinking. Since his invitation is delivered with such brio, I can't say no without looking like a spoilsport. And anyway, the idea of standing at the bar of Lehmann's and getting drunk is pretty appealing. I throw the calculator onto the table—I've just been putting myself through hell with it over the Kosiek files—pick up my jacket, and off we go. It's only five o'clock, and Madame Farouche is still there. I call over to her so quickly that she has no chance of asking me any questions. "I'm off to a meeting outside the building. I won't be back."

The fresh air outside! The weather in the street! You forget what it's like when you're stuck in the office all day. I feel completely relaxed and slap Bellmann heartily between the shoulder blades with the palm of my hand, so that it hurts him a little, the old Judas. He'd be the first to benefit if—right now, let's say—something bad were to happen to me.

I wonder briefly whether I should tell him all this, but decide against it because he isn't the type who would give a straight answer. He'd start hedging around the subject—"never in my life," and so on—and then things would get embarrassing for *me*. He'd take it as an invitation to saw off the branch I was sitting on. I know something's brewing, but of course I don't have anything concrete, so I have to keep my mouth shut.

In Lehmann's everyone you'd expect is standing around, all the people you presumably find there at all times of the day and particularly at night—noisy people brandishing their cell phones and talking endlessly about meetings they're supposed to have somewhere or other, but in the end this is the only place you ever see them. If I happen to catch one of their names and make a mental note of it, I look him up in my computer at the bank to see if he's listed as a debtor. It's a pretty high success rate, but most of them are only small-scale debtors who just want to be able to pay for their suits, their cell phones, and their drinks in Lehmann's, without having to work too hard. I check each of them off as I go past—in my imaginary capacity as enforcer, at least. It has a certain charm, standing among these people at the bar and knowing that you could cut off supplies for each and every one of them in a moment, but you don't do it because you've knocked off for the day.

"A bit like being a hanging judge on vacation," I say to Bellmann, raising my glass. He doesn't get it, and I try to explain to him, but he doesn't like jokes about work. Presumably he's afraid the same weapon might be turned against him at some point. He's straight down the line, through and through. On the one hand we need people like that in our department, but on the other, nobody like that can expect to be allowed near complicated dealings whose resolution would win him the admiration of his boss. Complicated affairs like the Kosiek case, for example. The first two pints have warmed me up nicely, and I try to look at the positive side of the Kosiek case. If I did manage to loosen the Gordian knot, I'd be the hero of the day. But it would take more than two pints of Guinness to give me any lasting enthusiasm about such a feeble hope. Rumenich wouldn't have given me anything that I could have solved successfully, coming out of it all with flying colors. No, no, my defensive strategy, based around my report—the one that explains everything, annotates everything, clarifies and covers and accounts for everything, making everything intelligible while at the same time extricating my neck from the noose—is the only correct one.

Bellmann is droning on about his day. I'm starting to get seriously bored, as I can tell by the fact that I'm trying to count the short and greasy hairs protruding from his nostrils, when all of a sudden he mentions something that gets me interested: Furnituro Ltd. Bellmann has never been to my place, he doesn't even know my home address, so he probably doesn't know that "Period Furniture Paradise" happens to be in the building where I live. I had had a look at the case myself at one point, but it was soon passed on to Bellmann "for further administration," after I had discovered that the partners and directors of Furnituro Ltd. were nowhere to be found. The new owner of the shop was a certain Anatol—we hadn't even gotten ahold of his surname yet—although he was not "officially" connected to Furnituro Ltd. On those grounds he rejected our demand for 1.2 million with a frosty smile. So we applied the phrase "wait and see," Bellmann was given the file, and I actually expected never to hear anything about it ever again. But Bellmann had gotten down to work in the meantime.

"You remember, there's our friend Anatol, who's set up with a certain Uwe. We know Uwe as well. A few years ago he had a fitness and Tae Kwon Do center that bit the dust, receivership and all the trimmings. But he's clean this time, he has a fitness center in the same building called Ladies Only, and that seems to be working."

"And?"

"I want to get proof that Anatol isn't just dealing in copies of period furniture because he has a passion for them. I want to prove that he's a front man for the people behind Furnituro Ltd. If I'm successful, we might be able to identify him as the de facto business manager."

"What kind of business would we be talking about?"

"No idea, but if I get authorization for a private detective, I'll find out."

That, of course, is a question directed at me. Strictly speaking, I'm his superior. I would have to authorize a private detective to carry out investigations against a debtor; no one else could. With debts amounting to 1.2 million, that wouldn't be a problem, but something keeps me from doing him that favor. I don't know why, but for a very brief moment there I had the feeling I was going to have to keep Bellmann away from Anatol and Uwe. Why might that be? I don't even know them. They're run-of-the-mill bank debtors, nothing strange about that. Is it because I live in the same building as they do? Am I getting sentimental? No, it must be something else. It's a very clear destructive impulse. I don't like the idea of the bank bankrupting Anatol and Uwe. I say to Bellmann:

"A detective? You'd have to give me something more than a few vague suspicions. I'd never get it past them otherwise."

He knows as well as I do that I don't have to get anything past anybody, because I'm ultimately responsible. He tries to hide his unease, unsuccessfully. I wonder whether this was why he invited me out, whether he just wanted to get me to authorize a detective, to show me that he was attending to his task with the proper commitment. The longer I puzzle over it, the more resolute I am. Anatol and Uwe are really in luck. The evening's over. Bellmann's given up. We down our third beer, and that's it.

14

The employee's classic reaction to growing pressure from his superiors is insomnia. Believe me: in this sense I am reacting in the classic manner to the transfer of the Kosiek case. I am sitting in the living room at two in the morning, completely exhausted and yet unable to sleep. The television is on with the sound turned down as I flick absently through *It's a Lovely Day Today*. Absently. It sounds domestic, well ordered. But it's nothing more than a vague hiss in my head, like the hiss on the television at sign-off used to be, when they still had sign-off.

I regret not having brought any files home. That was careless of me. That thing I said to Marianne wasn't a joke. The files lead an independent life, which is hostile to human life. Rumenich is pursuing me with memos. She puts these in the form of short, precise questions. Madame Farouche brings them to me from my signature file. I'm amazed at Rumenich's detailed knowledge of the Kosiek portfolio. She asks and asks. Herr Schwarz, what do you say about the difficulties of overinsurance where this property and that are concerned?

I look for the file, which I don't know of, which I've never heard of, in the mountain of files that Bellmann has dumped in my room. The portfolio was begun in 1965, a year after I was born. I didn't know there was a problem. No one ever mentioned it. But it's my task to know every detail in these—how many hundred?— files. Each one contains countless such details, but how are you supposed to tell the insignificant from the insignificant if you don't know what's in the others, if you're not familiar with all the rest?

Rumenich sends me these one-, two-, or three-liners, sometimes four, five, or six a day. I don't talk to her about it, or rather

she doesn't talk to me about it, but if I happen to bump into her in
the corridor I immediately launch into complicated explanations:
"I'm sure you'll give me all that in writing, in a thorough and com-
prehensible form. There's no point talking about details now—is
there?"

Of course. Of course not. I go back into my room, and a few
minutes later in comes a new memo with a new question that I don't
know how to answer. They are murderous little messages, the ones
Rumenich sends me. Their true content is always unspoken: "I'll get
you, Schwarz, I'll get you; you see how I'm collecting my strength?
You see how pointless it is to try and defend yourself?"

I prepare outlines and realize that each solution I try to put
together brings up more new problems. I try to incorporate these in
my formulation, and of course each fresh variant opens up more
variants that have to be pondered and dealt with. I start to feel I'm
standing on solid ground. I'm getting down to the basics. I'm getting
bold! Only to discover that in a file from 1978, which catches my
eye, a colleague has made a few handwritten notes in the margin
that tell me my original considerations were completely incorrect,
completely untenable, precisely because these considerations failed
to take notice of these handwritten observations that demonstrate
the precise opposite of what I had up to now suspected—and I have
to admit now, I realize, that my suspicions were pretty random.

There are days when I really have plenty of confidence in
myself and my analytical abilities when I've slept well and had a
good breakfast. Then I go into the office with the firm intention of
making the Kosiek case less terrifying, but the more resolute and
energetic I am in the morning, the more devastating the end result
in the evening. Once more I have failed to provide incontrovertible
results. At best I've managed a few sketchy proposals, all of which
look thoroughly provisional.

Now I'm really not so naïve as to imagine that Rumenich has
power over me, over the whole of me, I mean, that she could destroy

me, that she may even be doing so—but that's exactly how I feel. Whenever my colleagues in my department talk about the Kosiek case they often use the phrase "momentum of its own," or sometimes "incredible momentum of its own." They utter these words, it seems to me, terribly respectfully. I'm slowly beginning to understand why.

But I have no choice. Rumenich would ask me straight out what I think I'm doing in the bank if I'm not ready to work on the Kosiek case, and from the bank's point of view that question would be entirely justified.

In short, I'm sitting in our living room at two o'clock in the morning and trying to make sensible notes to myself, trying to get some clarity. Clarity! The very word is filled with such bitter mockery that it gives me stomach pains. When I was lying in my bed before, unable to sleep, I thought I'd get up and think through some more Kosiek-related problems and make some notes. I thought, I've got more or less all of the Kosiek-related problems in my head. But of course this is a terrible mistake. Without the files it's impossible. I am really, truly looking forward to going into the office tomorrow, to my files—I'm talking about *my* files, did you notice that? As long as I have the files, as long as I'm near them, I still have a chance of clarifying everything, of putting everything in convincing order, developing brilliant analyses, incisive suggestions. Don't I?

But even if I can't seriously do anything now, at night in my living room and without my files, there's still no point even thinking about sleeping. I have to stay awake. If I'm to achieve anything convincing in the Kosiek case, I'm going to have to keep my head together. But that's exactly what's causing me difficulties. Recently, more and more careless mistakes have been creeping in. No one notices that apart from me, and perhaps Madame Farouche, who is, thank you very much, obliged to say nothing. But it irritates me anyway. My brain no longer works the way it did. Whatever I try to do, I now find myself wondering if it could be used against me. I never used to think that. In *It's a Lovely Day Today* it says that this way of thinking—fearing possible accusations from other people, anticipating that a case might go wrong—is negative. Anyone who thinks that way magically attracts all the available crap, so to speak. I don't need any proof for this thesis. I'm just convinced by it. I don't really *believe* I can win in the Kosiek case. I'm still clearheaded enough to know that it's *impossible*.

I stare like a reptile at the silently flickering screen. I keep hopping through the ninety-nine channels we have. There's nothing that could hold my attention for more than five seconds. I sit in the living room until four o'clock. I decide to take a shower and get dressed and, earlier than usual—at five or half past—to go to the office. Then I go to sleep on the sofa. Marianne wakes me at seven. She shakes my shoulder and asks, "What's *this* all about?" I go to the bathroom. I feel as if I've got an ax buried in my skull.

15

Marianne and I get home from the office at the same time, nine o'clock in the evening. Her appearance immediately gets on my nerves. Completely drawn, all her prettiness gone, everything left in the office, with her clients, with Werner. I know I'm being unfair, I don't look much better myself—but is that of the slightest importance at the moment? Enjoying the malice in my voice, I ask her, "What have you got there?" I point in turn at the corners of her eyes. She's got running mascara there, but I want to *hear* her say it.

"What have I got where?" she replies loudly, straining to keep control of herself, I notice: she's recharged herself, too.

"There, on your eyes. Is it dirt?"

We are still standing by the door to the apartment. Marianne opens the door. We're inside. She goes to the bathroom and says, "Bastard."

I'm hurt. I try to follow her into the bathroom. She notices and closes the door.

I go to get a beer out of the fridge. There's none there, so I sit down in front of the television. Marianne comes out of the bathroom. She's taken off her makeup and looks old, ill, the way women look in the hospital. She asks, "So, what's for dinner?"

"Order us a pizza."

"You order it."

I don't want to make things worse, so I go ahead. Fine, two pizzas, four beers. They'll be here in a quarter of an hour. We should talk.

"What's up with you?"

"What do you think's up with me?"

"You're so irritable."

"Irritable? Me? Don't make me laugh. You're the one who's about to explode."

"Oh, stop it. I just want a bit of peace and quiet."

"He wants peace and quiet! It's enough to make you scream!"

"Please don't scream. That'll do, it really will. What's wrong with you?"

"Oh, you know, nothing. It just looks like I'm going to lose my job."

"How come? They just made you account manager a few weeks ago!"

"So? And a few weeks later I'm out. 'Success is a daily issue,' as the Americans say. Get that?"

"Oh bullshit."

"Yeah, bullshit, sure."

"So what's the problem?"

"I've fucked up, I've fucked up good and proper."

"Can you just tell me what's happened?"

"The hamburger account. The posters left the printers today, they've been distributed. Tomorrow they're going to be on every wall, every billboard."

"So?"

"I had them approved over the phone. But even before I did that, I spotted that our agency's name was spelled wrong at the edge. I told them the poster was fine, but they had to change that one thing."

"I see."

"I should have done it in writing, but I did it over the phone."

"So what's the problem?"

"The problem? Obviously the printers deny that I ever said the name was spelled wrong. It's all my fault. It's the biggest campaign the agency has ever taken on. And I, the account manager, made sure that their name was spelled wrong on those damned posters. Hello? Employment Agency?"

"Did Werner say anything about it?"

"He called me in. He had his assistant call me in. He never does that. He talked to me very quietly, as if he was consoling me. When I saw his face, I knew all at once that I was out."

"Out?"

"Of course he didn't say that. Strictly speaking, he didn't say anything at all. But it's clear as day. It's so completely obvious that you and I have to talk about it."

"And what are you going to do now?"

"No idea. Go back in tomorrow. Put my stuff in order. Wait and see what happens. I'm not going to resign, of course. I'm going to wait for the letter with my severance package."

"And you're not going to fight?"

"Fight? For what? My job? You can't be that naïve, not with the job *you* do. If I'd taken a few thousand marks out of the office safe and ended the campaign successfully, Werner would have come to some arrangement with me. But spelling his agency's name wrong, on the biggest and most important campaign he's ever done? No way, José!"

"As a matter of fact that's very funny, I . . ."

Just as I've finished saying "funny," Marianne leaps to her feet, her features blur, she bursts, really bursts, into tears and runs sobbing into the bedroom. I can't deny that I envy her. That's right, I envy her. Marianne has no idea that it'll be my turn in a few days' time. The infuriating, utterly pointless work on my memo is the only thing that's keeping me off the street, to put it rather dramatically. Marianne has always seen things in clear-cut terms. For someone like me, who's been pining away unredeemed for weeks in some indeterminate no-man's-land, that way of looking at things seems to have a liberating simplicity. I've still got my chance, which isn't really a chance at all.

Once her tears have subsided, I hear Marianne disappearing into the bathroom. I should go to her and comfort her, I know. But I don't feel like it. It has less to do with her than you might think. It has more to do with our life so far, in this apartment, which now looks to me as though it belongs to someone else. The people who live here are a youngish, high-income, childless couple with enough taste and money to arrange things the way they want to have them. And we are no longer that couple.

I always knew it would happen. It wasn't just cheap pessimism. Provisionality is built into the system we've chosen for ourselves. What did Marianne say? Success is a daily issue. That used to be an advertisement in *The Wall Street Journal*, if I remember correctly. They should know. What they say applies here, too, a long way from Wall Street. People like us get paid very well for a certain period of time, to accomplish certain tasks. Then, just before they establish themselves, they're replaced by other people, new people, who are a bit hungrier, a bit less expensive, a bit further from the idea of being important, of calling the shots. Other people do the running, just as we did the running three or four years ago. I don't find anything terrible about that. The only surprise is that the time has clearly come for that transition to take place. And of course it's a surprise that Marianne's the first to go. I always thought she was particularly fit, particularly adaptable and competent. Apparently her time has its limits as well.

The pizzas come. A friendly man, from some country somewhere in the world that offers him so little to live on that he thinks the five marks an hour that he makes here is adequate pay for his labors, hands them over to me. I give him what he probably considers a decent tip. I don't usually give tips. I cut off a corner of my pizza, pick up a beer, and sit down in front of the television. There's a dating program on, and I watch it keenly.

16

Writing a comprehensive report about something as complex as the Kosiek case requires courage, skill, a refusal to be intimidated, and a clear head. Qualities that I have, to a large extent, lost during the course of my work.

I speak into my Dictaphone. I talk myself blue in the face, thinking about Rumenich. I've seen her dictating, I've watched her, I thought it was exciting, it's like elegant swordplay in a cloak-and-dagger movie. She jabbers away nineteen to the dozen and has an almost spiritual facial expression. You can tell that she's imagining, down to their smallest details, the recipients of these memos who are about to discover they're headed for the scrap heap. She's excited, her cheeks are flushed, she's brilliant, her opponents haven't a chance. I try to imitate the way she dictates. My eye flies across the stacks of handwritten notes that I've prepared over the past few weeks—but can't get it to *take off* the way Rumenich does. I pretend to myself that I am doing it, I convince myself that my performance is incisive where it's actually questionable. I'll have to put my notes on Rumenich's desk tonight. She wants them first thing tomorrow, and she's going to discuss them with me the day after.

A few hours later I'm exhausted and I've finished my work. The memo is complete. Madame Farouche has typed everything out. It's an impressive stack of paper, altogether about fifty pages. I'm pleased and spare myself the final corrections. I ask Madame Farouche to hand my work to Rumenich's secretary with my best wishes.

Then I set off for the office party. A woman from human resources, a certain Frau Zwängler, is celebrating her fiftieth birthday in the basement, where the company holds its parties. She sent me a very cordial invitation via the company email. So of course I have to be there. On the way to the basement I feel an almost ludicrous sense of relief rising up in me. I've sorted out the Kosiek case! I've actually done it! Rumenich, of course, will find something dubious or even plain wrong in my report. But at the moment that isn't of the slightest importance. I've conquered the nightmare that's been hanging over me for the past few weeks, that's all that counts. No more Kosiek. This party is my party. I'm one of the last people to get to the basement. I see Bellmann, I see Rumenich, I nod to each of them in a businesslike way and set about finding something to drink.

Frau Zwängler has made a fruit punch for the party, and it's been cheerfully fermenting away. I notice the guests quivering with repulsion at every sip, but of course no one says anything. No one wants to get too close to the birthday girl. Incidentally, that seems to be old Zwängler's fate—that no one wants to get too close to her. Maybe it has something to do with the fact that she's the manager of human resources. She herself has no control over firings and disciplinary measures, but she does enforce them, and her whole manner gives the clear impression that she does it whenever the mood takes her. She's a spinster and by now, by her fiftieth birthday, she's an "old maid," as she has already announced more than once in the ten minutes I've been here.

I can't really explain that, because she's not actually all that bad-looking, apart from the fact that she's fifteen years older than I am, but even so, Frau Zwängler isn't someone I'd look at twice.

At some point later in the evening I find myself sitting next to her, me on the left, Bellmann on the right, and Zwängler in the middle, with me chatting across her bosom to Bellmann about enforcement cases, while at the same time knocking back one fruit punch after the other, like Bellmann and everyone else at the table. In between drinks I go on talking and talking over the—not all that bad-looking—bosom of Frau Zwängler, and I smell the flesh of Frau

Zwängler, warmed up by all the laughing and drinking and partying, and at some point—at the very same moment I become aware of how completely impossible what I'm doing is—I reach my right hand down to Frau Zwängler's left knee, to rub or stroke it, and Frau Zwängler lets me, without so much as a twitch. So I go on doing it and, with my right hand, I rub her left knee, which still feels pretty powerful, as does her thigh, which I work my way up slowly, inch by inch, tactfully trying to avoid hitching her skirt up. I'm almost insensible with all the fermented fruit punch and this thing I'm doing and—the climax of loss of control—I've really started to feel attracted to this woman.

And then it happens: Bellmann, who doesn't normally smoke, but who's smoking this time, and is clearly unused to holding cigarettes, accidentally drops his under the table and jumps after it so quickly that, in my surprise, I don't get my hand off Frau Zwängler's leg quickly enough. My first fear, of course, is that Bellmann will immediately make his discovery public and yell across the table, "Schwarz has his hand on Zwängler's knee!" or something equally bold. He doesn't do that, but the relief is only temporary, because his malicious smile tells me that he isn't going leave matters there.

So my lust has literally abandoned me, while at the same time I seem to have, just as literally, unleashed that lustful feeling in Frau Zwängler. Although, or perhaps because, I am now keeping my hand firmly away from her knee, her hand now seeks and finds my knee, and rubs it in a demanding and painful way. I sit stock-still, which Frau Zwängler takes as a challenge to resume her efforts more emphatically than before, kneading my whole knee black and blue. Meanwhile Bellmann won't stop grinning at me in that apparently conspiratorial way. It doesn't escape him, either, that it's now Frau Zwängler who's making a pass at me, and I try to suggest to him, with my expression of indifference, that I think it's all utterly grotesque, and there's nothing I can do about it, but he knows that I was the one who set Frau Zwängler off in the first place.

Nothing more happens in the course of that evening, which ends with everyone present hellishly fruit-punch-drunk. I also notice that at the end Frau Zwängler has managed to get ahold of a foreign desk manager who actually seems willing.

Bellmann shares a taxi to my place because I'm no longer in a fit state to drive on my own. I feel like puking, and I'm terribly ashamed in front of him. Did I really succumb to Frau Zwängler's erotic aura? Does Frau Zwängler *have* an erotic aura? The extent of my self-humiliation is apparent not in Bellmann's discovery of my sexual peccadillo, completely unimportant in itself, but in the fact that I clearly *needed* to get my hand up the old bag's skirt. I wanted to hurt myself, as badly as possible, and I managed that outstandingly, I think, as I stare glassily out of the taxi window to avoid having to look at Bellmann or talk to him.

He drops me off at the door of my flat, where Marianne is waiting for me.

I sway past her into the bathroom, where I spew pint after pint of half-digested fruit punch into the toilet bowl. Marianne comes in after me and holds my head.

17

A windy day. I step out into the morning with that stimulating sense of uncertainty and expectation that always comes when one is setting off on a long journey. I'm late. I was supposed to have a meeting with Rumenich at half past nine—a discussion of my report on the Kosiek case—but I didn't go. I'm going only now, and it's half past ten. Marianne asked me, "Shouldn't you be getting up?" and I screwed myself down into my pillows for another two hours, and she soon gave up trying to wake me. She went to her goddamned agency. God knows what she's trying to do there. Now I go into my goddamned bank and know exactly what to expect: Rumenich with her doubtless impeccably staged performance of *The Firing of Thomas Schwarz*, final act. I couldn't deny myself the pleasure of putting her nose out of joint by being appallingly late. My steps are light now. I'm the man who's late, so late that he no longer has to worry about whether he can still make that appointment, that crucial meeting. I know I'm fair game, so why should I be bothered that the sole purpose of my being there is to be declared fair game by Frau Rumenich? Never before have I gone to the bank in the certainty that I no longer belonged there. A highly amusing, apparently frivolous sensation—that's right, frivolity is exactly the right word for it. This sense of flippancy mounts the closer I get to Rumenich's room—first of all, subway stop by subway stop, then step by step, across the streets, up the stairs, finally along the corridors leading to her headquarters, from where she "made this department what it is today," as she has recently taken to stressing.

Her confidence has grown, and there are good reasons for that, since she, the stopgap lady, was the one who managed to eliminate me, the longtime candidate for the post of department head. Congratulations!

I walk in, straight into her office, without knocking, but not brashly, not rudely. I don't want a confrontation, I'd be bound to come off the worst. She's sitting behind her desk, over what I presume to be my report. She raises her head, and a smile, practically a conspiratorial smile, slides across her face. For a moment she holds her breath as though considering whether to send me outside and have my secretary bring her back in again, and then she offers me a chair. I say I'd rather stand, thank you. I know exactly what she's going to say now.

She's going to say, *Herr Schwarz, I've had a word with the company directors.*

"Herr Schwarz, I've had a word with the company directors."

She's going to say, *I've been intensely scrutinizing your work in the Kosiek case, and it seemed to me that the results were worthy of further discussion amongst those in charge.*

"I've been intensely scrutinizing on your work in the Kosiek case, and it seemed to me that the results were worthy of further discussion amongst those in charge."

"Intensely scrutinizing" is a lovely turn of phrase, Frau Rumenich—I think, but don't say. I don't want to make it easier for her than it is already.

It isn't easy for anyone with a responsible position in this company to say this openly. You yourself are in a responsible position, so you know what I mean. What I want to say is this: your treatment of the Kosiek case has caused a very great amount of unease.

"It isn't easy for anyone with a responsible position in this company to say this openly. You yourself are in a responsible position, so you know what I mean. What I want to say is this: your treatment of the Kosiek case has caused a very great amount of unease."

"Unease," I mumble, and unfortunately at this point I look down at the floor like a little boy getting a tongue-lashing.

You were expected to solve this case, Herr Schwarz. Instead you have given the bank—after weeks of work, let it be known—a piece of writing that amounts to nothing more than a list of the problems. Problems that are all recorded in the files, do you understand?

"You were expected to solve this case, Herr Schwarz. Instead you have given the bank—after weeks of work, let it be known—a piece of writing that amounts to nothing more than a list of the problems. Problems that are all recorded in the files, do you understand?"

She goes on talking in this manner, in this tone, and I notice that I'm starting to grin now, like a naughty schoolboy receiving an admonition that he doesn't take seriously. I can't separate what she's saying from what I'm imagining her saying, because they're always exactly the same.

Herr Schwarz, all in all, I have to tell you that company management has decided to give you the opportunity to find a new professional direction.

"Herr Schwarz, all in all, I have to tell you that company management has decided to give you the opportunity to find a new professional direction."

Now it's becoming absolutely revolting, because of course I have to play the game myself if I'm not to be fired. I say, "Well, that's not entirely welcome, as you may know, but of course I accept the challenge."

And as though we were discussing a project in which we were both involved, I continue in a committed tone: "What sort of time frame were you thinking about?"

As soon as possible, Herr Schwarz.

"As soon as possible, Herr Schwarz."

Fine, as soon as possible it is, then, I think.

"Okay, I think I'd best concentrate on my new duties while I'm clearing out my desk. I'd do best finding my new direction at home, don't you think?"

To put it as clearly as possible, Herr Schwarz. Until the end of your contractual notice you are free, and the severance payment that is usual in these cases will be paid to you.

"I'm really sorry, Herr Schwarz. But you must admit that there's nothing for you in this company as long as I'm here."

Hello? Did I hear that wrong? I'm not sure. What did she say? I mumble, just to be on the safe side, "Yes, of course, you're right," and see that Rumenich considers the discussion at an end.

I, too, have to admit that the case is fairly straightforward, and say, "Okay, then!" and leave Rumenich's office rather awkwardly. She prefers not to look after me as I go, but rather to rearrange important papers on her desk.

I never imagined it would be so simple.

18

So: I've been fired. The worst thing at the moment is that I have this thought buzzing around in my head and can't get rid of it. "You've fired me because I'm not thirty anymore." It's sung by a throaty male voice in that utterly phony tone that German pop singers have made their own. Apart from that, of course, the lyrics are complete twaddle. No one gets fired because he isn't thirty anymore. I'm in my mid-thirties, after all, and I'm being fired. You get fired because you fucked up. They say. But even that's not true. You get fired because other people decide to fire you, because they agree that somebody's got to go, and he goes.

I come back from Rumenich's office with a taste like sawdust on my tongue and can't get that thought out of my head. It's the kind of dreadful song you get coming out of jukeboxes at beer stands. Twenty years old or more, forgotten long ago, but still good enough to set some old drunks at the bar off crying and drinking some more, and pouring out their hearts to the old girl behind the bar, who doesn't want to hear any of it, anyway. Yes, that's how it's going to be. I'm going to be standing at Helga's beer stand in my greasy old Calvin Klein suit at ten o'clock in the morning, telling her, over my eighth little bottle of digestive bitters, that what happened to me was a terrible injustice, that there was this woman, Rumenich, who kicked me out of the orbit of my success, that everything would otherwise have been completely different, and so on and so on.

And these are just dumb old clichés, as we know. Everyone has the chance to get up, even after the bitterest defeat, and say, "It's a lovely day today!" Yes, that's the way to look at it. If Rumenich fires me, it's just the starting signal for my new life! I'm happy, I'm free! It's not going to be easy to sell Marianne my dismissal as a success story, but I'll get there. Or will she see me as a failure? That, or something like it, is what any unemployed person is supposed to think, that he's a "failure." I'll lie next to Marianne in bed, and I won't respond to her attempts to seduce me. Instead I'll stare at the ceiling, chain-smoking, and at some point I'll moan, "You deserved something better than me."

That's bullshit, too. Where do I get these images in my head from? Television? The papers? God knows; these images have accumulated over decades of hard and detailed work. It's all nonsense. The important thing now is to adopt some positive images, think clearly, act flexibly, recognize and exploit opportunities. When I walk into my office and close the door behind me—lock it, I turn the key in the lock—a sob wells up in me, something I hadn't expected, which overwhelms me as though it didn't come out of my own body but from somewhere outside. I weep the way I last wept as a child, but I take care not to be noisy about it. Madame Farouche mustn't hear anything. I want to leave as her boss, not as a beaten man.

I must blow my nose. I look for a handkerchief. I can't find one, snort back the snot, and call in Madame Farouche over the office intercom, asking her to bring some tissues. I depend on her not noticing anything. I'll just turn to the side. I see her lowering the door handle and, at almost exactly the same time—presumably with her head—knocking at the door. There's a moment's embarrassed silence, then comes her call of complaint: "Herr Schwarz, you've locked the door."

Uncertainty in her voice. I've never locked the door before, never in the four years I've been here.

"Oh, you're right, I forgot. I'll just open up."

I try to make it sound casual and innocuous, but she must have something wrong with her hearing if she can't hear what's up. I open the door. She looks at me and says, "Herr Schwarz, you look as if someone had . . ."

"—just fired me?"

"No, that's not what I was going to say. Has something happened?"

She looks so unfazed that I'd swear she knew everything, that she'd possibly known for days.

"Now, I really only wanted to tell you in a quarter of an hour, but if you ask me like that: Yes, Frau Rumenich has, with immediate effect, released me from all my duties."

"Released you?"

"She's given me the sack!"

Madame Farouche hands me the tissue I'd called her about. I keep my composure, blow my nose. She watches me, not particularly astonished. I'm sure she knew before I did.

"You must have gotten wind of what was coming."

"Me? Why would I? Please!"

"Whatever, it doesn't matter. Just make sure that you come out of this okay!"

She storms off, terribly insulted. I've never insulted her in four years, but I have now. Nothing matters anymore, and the lying bitch can go hang.

A classic scene follows, one that I know so well from countless television soaps that I wonder if it's really happening to me. I pack up my things. There isn't much, an incredibly small amount, in fact, when you think that I've spent four years in this office, but I seem to have left hardly any visible traces. When I pick up Marianne's picture in the little sterling silver frame, another sob escapes me. She's going to laugh at me, that much is certain. Of course she'll act hurt at first when I tell her, and she'll agree with me in condemning Rumenich and the bank—but she won't be able to resist the satisfaction that things aren't going a bit better for me than they are for her. I know that feeling too well to believe anyone could ever be immune to it. I mean that wonderful sense of superiority that everyone feels when they're faced with a failure who's obliged to expose himself. You don't have to be a sadist to be delighted when someone else goes to pieces. The underlying principle of our existence is the exclusion of others. Everyone is a potential adversary who might take something away from us, so we're delighted when he gets caught. It's perfectly normal. Even Marianne's sympathy would be faked.

I've packed my things together in a briefcase. I look around, trying to find something that would stop me from going, but I can't find a thing. I'm really through with everything here. I step out into the corridor. I see Madame Farouche in her room, her face a mixture of horror and a craving for excitement. We don't exchange glances. I decide to say nothing, not a word of farewell, it would just be nonsense, anyway, and I expect I'd get abusive.

It's midday, the bank people are going to lunch. I move among them, in the corridors, in the elevator, in the lobby, in the street. The others at the bank quite naturally consider me one of their own. I'm grateful to them for that, so grateful. I feel a certain tenderness for them because they don't know I'm out. If they did, I imagine they'd probably be on me in a split second, tearing my clothes off my body and dividing them up among them.

Out of the bank, into the subway, midday. Nobody goes home at this time of day, unless they've just been fired without notice. I reach our apartment. I feel as though I've entered illegally. I walk around and look at everything. I ask myself what a bailiff could take away, and see a whole lot.

19

Marianne and I are sitting in the kitchen. It would be obvious what had happened even if we hadn't already talked about it, and a warm, fundamentally human atmosphere fills the room. The solidarity of two defeated people who know that no one can disturb their unity, at least not for this evening.

Marianne runs me through the conversation she had with Werner, in every single detail. She leaves out the conclusion at first, but I know it anyway. She makes an effort to stress what is humorous in her account of events. How the tip of Werner's nose moved while he talked, for example, how he tried to find the most innocent-sounding turns of phrase and literally broke out sweating.

Marianne is cooking medallions of pork in a white-wine sauce. I'm making a fresh salad with sweet corn, avocado, cucumber, tomatoes, and carrots. Finally she bursts into tears and admits that she, like myself, has been dismissed from her job with immediate effect. She quickly regains her composure. We laugh—what a coincidence!—and go on cooking.

Now it really gets romantic. We talk about our situation as though we were members of a conspiratorial sect. Like two people who have been involved with each other, unaware that they belonged to the same organization. We talk about the fact that we'll both have to go on the dole, and we have some fun repeating that hated word. We calculate that between us we have about five thousand marks in all—enough money to go on living as we've been doing for a little while. Without work, though—that's over and done with. They can all fuck off, the whole bunch of them!

We go to bed and, once we're lying down, we get into an

argument, filled with almost entirely destructive hatred, about who's going to turn the light out.

The next morning Marianne reveals that she's decided to go to her aunt Olivia's for a while. She tells me this over breakfast, quite matter-of-factly, in a reasonable tone, with a lowered voice, meaning: no debate. I oblige. In a way I'm relieved at the idea of being free of Marianne for a while.

"You'll see, it's the best thing for both of us at the moment," she says, wanting more than a mere acknowledgment. What she wants is my agreement, and that's not something I'm going to give without a fight, as she ought to have figured out.

"If you really think the best thing for us is to leave each other in the lurch in a situation like this . . ." I hear myself saying, apparently gravely insulted. I'm not really insulted at all. I'm glad she's going.

"We'd just drag each other farther down."

"Ah, so I drag you down."

I can't be childish enough.

"I didn't say that."

"Yes, you did. But off you go to your worldly-wise Olivia. She won't be able to help you, either."

"I'm not saying she will, not the way you mean. But at least at her place I'll be able to think along different lines."

"Different lines! As if thinking along *different lines* would be any use to you now!"

"As a matter of fact it would!"

And so on, and so forth. We manage to drag this utterly half-written dialogue on for over an hour, just as hopeless at the end as it was at the beginning, and with neither of us standing up and slamming the door as we leave the room. Then the conversation ebbs away. Marianne says she still has to pack. I say I'm going to have to take care of the kitchen on my own from now on, and start loading the dishwasher.

We sleep side by side in our bed for the last time, and in the morning I take her to the station. She says she loves the station, and traveling in general. I declare traveling to be the most pointless distraction in existence. She gets on the train, and we don't even give each other a farewell kiss, we just shake hands. I can't make her out behind the mirrored glass, I can't see her sitting down in her seat, I can't see whether she looks at me or whether she ignores me completely. That gives me the right to leave right away, without waiting for the train to pull out. It's like a farewell forever, an irrevocable parting. I'm certain that I won't see Marianne again in a week, maybe not even in two or three, perhaps only in a few years' time in a divorce court.

In the station hall I turn around again, shivering even though it's warm. I'm sure that this is goodbye forever on Marianne's part, and I wait desperately for dramatic emotions to come. But there's nothing, apart from a vague sense of relief and a certain anxiety about my future—my future over the next quarter of an hour as I stroll through the city to reassure myself that absolutely nothing is going to stop me from moving around.

Absolutely nothing does. I walk, neither slowly nor quickly, through the red-light district that begins behind the main entrance to the station. It seems to be turning into a mild day, a gentle, warm wind is blowing. It's warm but not hot, completely innocuous weather. There's hardly anyone in the street in this part of town at this time of day. The hookers are sleeping it off, the bars closed ages ago and are in no great hurry to open up again. A few kebab stalls are getting ready for business, and the previous night's garbage is scattered on the pavements.

I've decided to visit Markus, the screenwriter. That time he told me about his separation from Babs I was secretly rather shocked at how easy it was for him, how little he seemed to feel. Now I see what he meant. I go there on foot. I want to take as long as possible to get there.

In my mind I go through some of the phases of my marriage to Marianne, the way you might walk the stations of the cross. We've given each other a present of the provisional ending, the crucifixion itself. On the other hand we've conscientiously traveled the *via dolorosa*, the passion. But what's passion, *dolor*, grief, in a context like this? Nothing remains but a few scenes over trivial matters. That's why everything, our whole lives, can be rearranged without the slightest trouble. We'll argue a bit about money, furniture, valuables, but more out of habitual self-righteousness than greed. We'll lose a bit of money, but that's not so bad. The only thing that really counts is the fact that we've both lost our jobs, both at the same time. I think it's obvious that once all this is over there will be no reason, however implausible, for us to stay together. Markus opens the door and raises his eyebrows when he sees me.

"What are you doing here?"

"Marianne's left me."

"But why aren't you at the bank?"

"Got the sack."

"I see. And I thought you'd come about the money."

"Don't worry about it."

"Come in, then. But I haven't much time, I'm writing."

"Could I have a coffee?"

"Sorry, I haven't got any in the house."

"Let me take you out for one."

"I've got no time at the moment, I really haven't. I have to get a draft ready by lunchtime. Maybe tomorrow, or the day after. Let's speak on the phone."

"Right. I thought a friend would have some time for somebody who'd just lost his job and his wife."

"You're joking."

"No joke."

"Okay, okay. But please, I really can't, not at the moment. I *will* have time, don't worry. Later. Let's speak on the phone, yeah?"

I understand, there's nothing to be done. And it really can wait until tomorrow or the day after or until I don't know when. What would Markus have to say to me, anyway? That the people in the bank are bastards and that I'll soon find another job. That Marianne wasn't right for me, anyway, and that there'll be another one to come along shortly who suits me much better. I can spell all that out for myself. I could even buy a men's magazine and study the tips on relationships. I could watch a daily soap on TV, there's bound to be a character with exactly my problems. I say, "Sorry to take you un-awares like that. You must think there's something else up. I'm just a bit up in the air, that's all."

"It'll sort itself out. Chin up!"

"Fine, I'll see you later."

"See you. Give me a call if there's anything you need."

On the stairs, as I'm leaving, a good mood suddenly comes over me. That conversation was so fantastically stupid that I burst out laughing. You just can't beat good friends. I walk home, to make this mood last longer.

20

Not far from our apartment there's a square that I knew existed, but nothing more than that. None of my daily journeys took me to it, and I had no reason to go there. I still have no reason to go there, but I'm there, anyway, because all of a sudden I have time on my hands. I've solved the question of clothes—how can I plausibly act like a businessman, walking through the city in the late morning while the whole world's at work—at a stroke. I wear a three-piece suit and a tie.

The center square is built around a bus station. There are shops around the outside. An optician, butchers, photography shops, a liquor store, supermarkets, banks. To my astonishment my former employer also has a branch here, which I discovered only today. Old and new buildings stand side by side, quite randomly. You'll find dozens of squares like this in every city in the world. Its meaning consists entirely in its function. There would be nothing to say about it if there weren't people walking around there. Lots of people, during working hours—and what people! Is there a home for the handicapped somewhere around here? I notice that by day there are considerable numbers of handicapped people in the street. Some of them have astonishing deformations, which I look at with veiled interest. These people certainly don't work. By law, for example, the bank must, like any business, employ a certain quota of handicapped people. These people are, whether mentally or physically handicapped, drawn to the kind of work they're capable of doing. But of course there isn't enough work for all the handicapped. Many of them have to be looked after by our mutually supportive society. These handicapped people draw benefits without having to do anything in return, and are free to wander around the stores at eleven o'clock in the morning.

Of course not all the people I see are handicapped—far from it, the handicapped might even form the smallest group, they're just the most conspicuous. There are tramps and homeless people, too, drunks and crazies stumbling around, and of course they're also conspicuous. But the most interesting group is the largest: a particular kind of people you'd probably describe as "normal," despite the fact that they aren't. They're neither mentally nor physically handicapped in the true sense of the word, and yet they have no social purpose, and never will. Only at second glance can you spot their defects. With some of them you can only guess. Most of them simply have an intelligence below the average, paired with a lack of social adaptability. These two factors, taken together, ensure that they are no use to anyone. But there are also individuals within this group who seem to have what it takes, and who are outsiders anyway. It's as though they have a particular gene missing, they lack a particular property and that makes them inadequate. I seem to be one of those. And that's why, as if today, I'm part of the freak show held every morning in this square. I'm a freak who, with his suit, his tanned face, his expensive shoes and manicured fingernails, looks for all the world like a bank director, although he's just become a hardship case. My appearance, my clothes, my manner all indicate a man who belongs to a social elite. The facts reveal that I am not such a man. My mimicry is my handicap, and if you think I could simply change my clothes, you haven't understood anything at all.

The people walking about in this square are my new gang. Starting today I'm one of them. Of course it can't be true, I think to myself. Of course I can simply escape to safety by going where I belong—into the branch of the bank.

As soon as I enter the service area I know I've committed a deadly blunder, but I can't go back. A young cashier, whom I once had as a trainee for three weeks in my department, has already seen me. He nods to me with that servile friendliness that we instill in our younger colleagues as the correct way of dealing with the general public. He asks the customer he's serving to wait for a moment and waves me, fairly discreetly, out of the short line of people waiting for him at the cash desk. I accept his invitation.

I find myself wondering whether I would have reacted the same way if I were still deputy manager of the department of foreclosure and liquidation. Or would I, without waiting for his invitation, have gone straight to the cash desk and called the boy over to me? The answer is: As deputy manager of the department of foreclosure and liquidation, I wouldn't be here. Quite unconsciously, the young man is taking the correct course of action: "Herr Schwarz! This is a surprise! What brings you here?"

Does he know something? He can't possibly. He'd be one of the last to find out anything at all. I reply, "I want to withdraw four hundred marks. Don't worry about it, I'll use the automatic teller."

"Please, Herr Schwarz, it won't take a moment."

I wonder whether I should suggest that he serve the other customers first. That would have been my duty as his superior, and I'm not that anymore, but I don't want to attract any attention; I want no discussion, no disturbance. I just want him to go quickly, so I let him get on with it. He enters my account number into the computer and looks at my data. I can tell from his face that he's struck by something. I say, "Well?"

He leans over the counter and whispers, "I see your salary hasn't been paid in this month yet. Do you want me to make inquiries?"

All of a sudden I feel the veins in my body dilating with anxiety, and say, "Let's just leave it, I've taken care of it already. The money will be coming in next week. There was a mistake in accounts."

He says, "Okay, that's different," and seems satisfied with my explanation. He prepares the payment of the four hundred marks. He walks a little way from his desk and talks to a colleague. I can't hear what they're saying. Presumably he's asking him if he's already had his wages or if he knows anything about a mistake in accounts. His colleague shrugs his shoulders and shakes his head. They both glance over at me. After a while the boy comes over with the four hundred marks and counts them out for me. He says, "I hope they take care of that problem in accounts."

I answer irritably, "I told you already. They've worked it out!"

We make formal goodbyes. He is as servile as his training demands. I'm as brash as might be expected of a deputy department manager. When I try to put the bills in my wallet as I leave, my hands start trembling so violently that I can't get them in. I scrunch them up in my fist and stick them in my trouser pocket.

Outside

21

The music's so loud it sets your guts vibrating. Uwe is clutching his key ring with the miniature Coke bottle and waving it around in front of the barmaid's face. When he catches her eye he points at our three empty whisky glasses. On a shelf at each of the three bars in the Funkadelic, Uwe has a bottle of Johnny Walker Black Label with his name on it. As he explained to me, only a few customers can claim to enjoy that privilege.

The barmaid—a pretty slut with a barbed-wire necklace tattooed on her neck, long, smooth, dyed-black hair, and a pale doll's face—pours each of us two fingers of whisky. When she's finished, Uwe takes a diagonally folded ten-mark note out of his clip, folds it lengthwise, and holds it out to her between his index and middle fingers. This is a tip, the drinks are already paid for.

Uwe's money clip is famous in the Funkadelic, and elsewhere, too, Anatol tells me. It's always about an inch thick, always with a thousand-mark note on top of the other notes. The barmaid grabs the ten-mark note and, without a word of thanks, turns around, her chin jutting out. There is no doubt that she *does not like* Uwe. He lights a cigarette with a plastic lighter in the shape of long, slim women's legs under a red miniskirt. He grins, lets the smoke escape from his mouth, sticks out his tongue, and gives a dirty laugh. Uwe is having a party, Anatol is joining in, and, if I'm seeing things correctly, I'm joining in, too.

When I was a student I used to spend a bit of time in discos. Always in the wake of my friend Markus, who had once been a major figure in the club scene—"numero uno," as he called himself. I understood the rules people operated by there, and standing next to Markus, I could feel hipper than I really was. But when I joined the bank none of that mattered anymore. Of course I used to go out in the evening now and then, but it was to the places bankers go to: Harry's New York Bar, Lehmann's, expensive and fashionable restaurants. Here in the Funkadelic the main players are *children*, people under thirty. The things they consider important are a particular kind of clothes, a particular kind of music, a particular kind of drugs, and a particular kind of pose. Perhaps they're not all that far off the mark on their own terms. But it isn't my kind of thing. I'm just here because of Uwe and Anatol, who are trying to show me that they know their way around here, even if they don't allow the young people's codes to apply to them. They act as though they're old masters of the scene, holding the scepters in their hands independent of any kind of fashion, simply because they've been around for so long.

The truth is this: you don't have to like Uwe to find him striking. His golden tan from his own solarium, his titanic body, pumped up in his own gym, his cropped, peroxided blond hair, make him look like a coarse and hulking twin of Van Damme—and he's over six foot three.

Anatol, on the other hand, is of rather average proportions. He wears a Hawaiian shirt and stonewashed jeans, and he wears his hair in a mullet.

As for me, the third member of the gang, I still like to wear my suits, even when I go out at night. It has advantages, you get treated better. Not because people think you're hip but because they think you're some kind of important person simply because you don't look as if you're there for fun. But anyone who isn't here for fun is either a cop or a criminal, doing deals of some kind. I'm neither of those things, but the fact that I'm wearing a suit and standing next to Uwe and Anatol is inexplicable in itself—so I look mysterious, and I like that.

It wouldn't be fair to say that Uwe and Anatol have done anything wrong, exactly; it's more that certain problems have arisen in their lives, and I may be able to help them with these, in an advisory capacity. That's why we're together.

Uwe puts his bare forearm around my shoulders. He is wearing a muscle shirt with the slogan: "If good looks don't count—don't count on me." He explains to me that there is always trouble in the Funkadelic.

"What kind of trouble?" I ask.

"Fights," he replies. He points toward a group of boys, four of them, standing near the dance floor.

"I've been keeping my eye on them for a long time now."

I'd never have noticed them. Perfectly normal boys in freshly washed jeans and ironed T-shirts, their hair cropped.

"Hooligans," says Uwe.

The Funkadelic has a pretty tight door policy, which is to say that not everyone who wants to gets in. Uwe says, "They're not here to dance."

And as if he'd given the signal, for no apparent reason the boys pick up some bar stools and start swinging them around. In a flash, and indiscriminately, they tear into the people on the dance floor. No one knows what's going on. The people who have been hit fall to the floor, blood sprays, bones break, women scream, men yell, the music stops. The enormous doorman, his assistants, *and* Uwe, who removes his arm from my shoulder, rush on to the dance floor and start flailing their fists. Then we have a one-minute Tae Kwon Do display from Uwe on the dance floor, in the course of which he punches out all four attackers. Uwe's fighting technique, his leaps, are impressive. He holds the tips of his fingers rolled in like claws. There's no aggression in his face as there usually is, just relaxed concentration. As you might imagine a killer at work. I assume that the pictures he sees in front of his eyes mingle in his brain with the ones that thousands upon thousands of kung fu films have left in his head. Anatol and I put one cigarette after another to our mouths and take turns lighting them. We don't say a word. This is hard-core fighting, with extreme violence on both sides. At some point the police and ambulance men turn up. Uwe, not fazed for a second by the fight, gives them the information and help they need. My knees turn to jelly, and I sit down on my bar stool. Customers are pushing their way to the exit. The defeated brawlers are arrested, the injured tended to, eyewitnesses questioned. Uwe comes back over to join us. After a while a man I take to be the Funkadelic's manager takes the microphone behind the DJ's desk and explains the situation. He's a huge man, apparently not even slightly disconcerted by what we've just seen. "What's just happened was terrible, but we're not going to let those guys spoil our party." The tone in which he says that is so flat that everyone understands: he doesn't think what happened *was* particularly terrible, and he doesn't think there's a party happening here. He just wants business to go on as usual.

But Uwe is a little out of breath. The casualties are carried off and the music starts up again, at the same lunatic volume. Our guts vibrate as before. Nothing has happened. Or has it? People pass and slap Uwe on the shoulder. He grins at me proudly—he's a hero, he's saved the evening, the whole Funkadelic, with the superior power of his muscles and his martial arts.

I have butterflies in my stomach and disappear to the men's room, where I shut myself in a cubicle to be alone for a while. I try to cry, but I can't. While I was still at the bank I never would have come across anything like that, I reflect. Nothing happened to me, I wasn't even involved in what happened, but the very fact that I was in a club where something like that was *possible* and obviously expected, makes me despair.

I emerge again and walk back to my seat, to my whisky. Uwe's feeling fantastic. I pat his shoulder. This is probably a big day in his life. It could even be quite a normal one to him. The manager comes over and shakes Uwe's hand. He's relaxed, not excited or gushy. He says, "We should work together sometime." Uwe points to Anatol and me and says, "He's my partner and he's my adviser." I smile as though I could imagine working with the manager, too, but he doesn't so much as look in my direction.

Uwe gives the barmaid a signal: Top up the whisky. She smiles and obliges. He gives her another ten-mark note, folded lengthwise, while I try to come up with an excuse for bringing the evening to a close, shaking off these new acquaintances, my new lifestyle, as quickly as possible. Nothing occurs to me. Uwe raises his drink to me, and we clink glasses.

22

On Monday morning I wake up early—far too early, given that I don't need to go to the office. My worker-self *urgently* wants to go to the bank, wants to send emails and faxes, make phone calls, hungers for validation at his desk. The fact that there is no longer a bank or a desk waiting for him sends him into a frenzied search, and the longer I stays in the kitchen after my hasty breakfast, the greater is his anxiety that he might miss his imaginary duties.

But that's not all. Much more depressing are the aftereffects of the fight in the Funkadelic last night, which I haven't finished dealing with.

When Uwe spoke to me in the hall, I should, after giving him an evasive answer, have simply have walked on. But I was too surprised that he talked to me at all, addressing me as an old friend as if it were the most natural thing in the world, because that was the way he talked to everyone.

"Hi, neighbor!" he bellowed down the ground-floor corridor, waving me over to him with his index finger one morning as I was coming out of the elevator and he was coming in through the front door, presumably from his gym. I laughed nervously and decided to respond to his greeting and his gesture as though they were entirely appropriate—if not to me, then at least to his own rudimentary notions of courtesy.

I walked over to him, genuinely amused. As usual I was wearing my business suit, and he, as usual, was wearing a muscle shirt—slogan: "Hot Muscles"—that revealed his half-naked torso.

I would have assumed that he was scared, or at least respectful, of people like me. After all, I looked exactly like the people in his bank, who could easily turn off the money supply for him and his gym. In fact I *had* worked at his bank, even if he didn't know that.

He spoke quietly, his voice familiar but not threatening: "Maestro, you look as if you could help me. Sorry to bother you in the middle of the hall like this, but I'm in a bit of a hurry."

What was I supposed to do? I could hardly exclaim: "I beg you, sir, desist!" And I did think there was a certain charm about the way he did it. Nonetheless it occurs to me: if I'd still been working at the bank I'd have gotten rid of him. I'd have had better things to do than accept this peculiar invitation to the office of his gym.

His office was a spacious, windowless room, lit by two neon tubes on the ceiling, with posters of Schwarzenegger and Van Damme. There were also pin-ups from American *Playboy* of Sable, an Amazon wrestler. My eye must have lingered a moment too long on them, because Uwe grinned and said, "She's not too bad, is she?"

"Okay. What do you want from me?"

"You know who Bellmann is?"

He was being incredibly informal, so I decided to do the same.

"And do *you* know who Bellmann is?"

"And how. He's been here already this morning and talked to me about you."

I didn't get it. I said, "I don't get it."

"Well, you are colleagues, aren't you?"

"*Were* colleagues."

Uwe looked at me. He appeared to be thinking.

"All the better," he said.

"Can you tell me what I'm supposed to be doing here?"

"This Bellmann isn't the sharpest knife in the drawer. Which isn't to say that he's not dangerous. He wants to pin something on me. I'll just say: Furnituro Ltd."

"Means nothing to me," I lied.

"I can imagine. It wouldn't mean anything to me if I were you. Sit down, and I'll tell you what's happening."

It turned out that this guy knew *everything* about Furnituro Ltd., he knew about everything the bank knew about him and Anatol, and he'd found it all out from Bellmann. Apart from the fact that he, along with Anatol, effectively *was* Furnituro Ltd., and Bellmann didn't know that. An awful idiot, that Bellmann, I'd always been sure of it. Of course Uwe wouldn't let me share in his knowledge without first telling me "what was up," without making it clear to me that I was going to be working for him. For money, of course.

"On the books?"

"Pff. Hardly."

"And how am I to help you?"

"Get rid of Bellmann."

Clearly, this was not going to be difficult. Bellmann had probably only called on Uwe out of embarrassment. I was impressed by Uwe's confidence. He knew very well that, since he had told me his story, I could squeal on him to the bank. But he knew I wouldn't. Why? Plenty of reasons. I would rather help Uwe against Bellmann than help the bank against Uwe and Anatol. Then we went over to "Period Furniture Paradise," where Anatol was sitting in his office. Uwe introduced me as his new adviser. Anatol greeted me warmly— and that was it. I felt a bit uncomfortable, but that subsided when Uwe pressed five thousand marks in cash into my hand.

"You don't have to do anything for this. It's just so you know I mean business."

I put the money in my pocket and went back up to the apartment. And I sat, somewhat flabbergasted, in my kitchen, put the five thousand down in front of me, and wondered what had really changed. And the answer was: nothing at all. Bellmann wasn't going to show up in the near future, and if he did, it would be easy— under the pretext that we had, after all, worked together—to throw him off the scent. It wasn't much in return for five thousand, it was really nothing at all.

The bad thing now, though, is that Uwe and Anatol have been calling me every day since then, wanting to meet. I never refuse one of these "invitations," because I'm worried about the trouble it might cause. They usually want to go to the Funkadelic, so that's where we go. There's endless backslapping and clinking of whisky glasses. Conversations generally revolve around who has the most money and muscles. It's revolting. You, yes, you, no doubt think your life has nothing to do with any of this. You're wrong, though. Your life, even yours, is all about money and muscles, in some way or another—if you're honest, you'll admit it.

It's midday. I toy, as I do every day, with the idea of calling Marianne at Olivia's, but I don't do it. And she doesn't call me, either, and perhaps it's an accurate reflection of our relationship—that horrible word!—that we think about each other without talking to each other. Disgusted with myself, I get to my feet and decide to go into town to buy a suit. I have an urgent need for a three-piece suit with eleven buttons on the waistcoat. I feel weak at the moment, but I'm going to do it, I'm really going to do it.

23

One ordinary weekday I decide I've suffered enough, and it's time to go to the supermarket in the grand style. Not any old supermarket, of course, but the one in the city, in the basement of a big department store that I used to visit regularly after long days in the office, to buy lobster and champagne for dinner, for Marianne and me. How I loved that image of myself: the young business guy in the evening, a bit tired but in good shape, with a loosened knot in his tie, his head still full of important work matters, buying delicacies for himself and his beloved. I used to imagine I must be an extremely attractive sight to the single young businesswomen who were also doing their shopping, and who were here in large numbers in the evening, and the idea really appealed to me, how they probably envied Marianne, even though they didn't know her.

Now, late in the afternoon, I set off to get that very same kick from the supermarket. It's actually a bit early, only half past five, but it doesn't matter, it'll be okay.

The glass doors part silently as I walk toward them: let the pleasure begin. I'm in a good mood, even in something of a state of euphoria at having such a brilliant idea as to come here after spending the whole day alone in my apartment, in a mood of genuine despair. The idea suddenly occurs to me: What if I've got no money? No, I have some, I feel for my wallet in my seat pocket, there it is. No, I don't need to worry, I know exactly what's wrong. I don't have that pleasantly exhausted feeling of relaxation that you have after a successful day in the office. I'm cramped, tense, my suit looks suspiciously fresh, and my face must, too.

I go and stand by the fish bar. I'll buy something delicious, not lobster necessarily, but maybe some prawns, or a sea bass. Two Asian people are standing ahead of me in line, talking excitedly about the fish tank behind the bar, clearly delighted that there are *living* fish swimming about in it. But in the end they opt for something else. I, on the other hand, want to see a fish dying. When my turn comes, I smile at the salesman and point to the basin behind him. The businesslike friendliness vanishes from his face at a stroke, as though I'd slapped him. His expression of concern is utterly at odds with the stupid costume that he and everyone else behind the fish bar have to wear, on the orders of his marketing director. A blue-and-white-striped linen apron, a red neckerchief, and a sailor's cap make the man, who must be in his mid-forties, look like an aging sea dog from the Baltic coast. I wonder what he's done with his life to end up wearing fancy dress behind a fish bar.

"I'd like a carp from the basin behind you," I say very politely, in an almost wheedling tone.

A little pained, he calls out the name of his colleague in the freezer room.

"Can't right now!" the voice replies.

So Cap'n has to battle with the carp all on his own. He yields to his fate, picks up a little net, and starts wiggling it clumsily about in the fish tank. The fish are suddenly in uproar. I wonder if I should tell him I wouldn't necessarily insist on carp, and that I'd just like whatever he happens to catch first. Then he does manage to net a decent carp. It must be over two feet long.

He hoists it out of the tank, leaving a great flood of water behind the bar. The carp flaps back and forth in the net with astounding force and almost manages to escape, but Cap'n keeps his free hand on it and somehow manages to splash the panicking creature into the metal bowl of the scale. He clutches it brutally by the throat and pointlessly asks me: "This one okay?"

The pointer on the scales flies back and forth like a windshield wiper.

"Fantastic," I reply.

Cap'n opens the lid of an appliance whose purpose I would not have known but immediately guess, and throws in the carp, shuts the lid, and turns a dial. A high-pitched whistling sound emerges. It's clear that this whistling does not bode well for the fish, which dies, I don't know how. Cap'n looks to the ceiling as though hoping for help. The whistling sound comes to an end, and Cap'n opens the machine and takes out the carp, which looks a little paler than it did. Its lips are swollen and, it seems to me, slightly singed. I decide it's probably been killed by an electric current.

"Gutted?" asks our nautical friend, and he's looking a little paler, too.

"Please."

I remember seeing Japanese sushi chefs dismembering fish so quickly, with rapid fingers and tiny knives, that it looked as though the fish were disintegrating into ideally proportioned little pieces all by themselves. But old Cap'n goes to work like a murderer. He slits open the carp's belly with a blunt-looking knife. The wound isn't clean, and the flesh is jagged. He gets annoyed because he knows I've seen it, he's aware that I know he's a dilettante. He plunges his fist inside the fish.

I say, "Watch out for the gallbladder."

Cap'n turns to me as though I had kicked him in the behind. His eyes are filled with sheer hatred. Great, that's just the way I like it.

"I have just one thing to say: I'm part-time here, and I'm not a goddamned fisherman or a goddamned fish butcher or whatever. I do my work the way I've been shown. You can't ask more than that for twenty marks an hour."

I'm delighted, and say, "Hey, I think you've misunderstood me. I asked you to watch out for the gallbladder. My advice didn't seem out of place under the circumstances. I had no desire to know your hourly wages. But if you want my honest opinion, I think you're very well paid for the job you're doing there."

"Now listen, don't you get funny with me."

"Funny? Who's being funny? I'd suggest that we have a chat with your manager."

"That can be arranged."

Cap'n is furious and goes to get his boss. I look around. There's a long line of very irritated people behind me. They don't care what the problem is. They want to get to the front and do their shopping. They're going to have to show a little patience. The manager comes. He's wearing his Baltic fisherman outfit as well. I explain to him that Cap'n Junior's evident lack of dexterity prompted me to advise caution with the bladder when gutting the fish. At this he had become quarrelsome. The manager calms me down and delivers a warning to Cap'n Junior. That makes me feel better. I reach toward the knot in my tie and deliver a furious speech about the failure of Germany's service industries. Now that I'm into my stride, I find it difficult to stop. Cap'n pretends to agree, Cap'n Junior humbly prepares the ragged fish, and I am just starting to get into the swing when the waiting mob behind me starts cursing. To my surprise their fury is directed at *me*, not at the two Cap'ns. They're telling me to shut up, clear out, that I have too much time on my hands, and so on.

In utter consternation I interrupt my speech, pick up my package of fish, and walk over to the cash register. I pay and walk numbly to the subway. I enter a crowded compartment of people going home from work. Before I get off, I slowly lower my arm and drop the packaged fish in among the feet of the passengers. Once I'm out, someone calls behind me, "You've dropped something!"

I don't turn around. He repeats, rather more urgently, "You've dropped something!"

I walk faster, I start running. The doors close. The train sets off. I run home and hope no one is carrying my fish after me.

24

Marianne, is that *you?*"

"Yes, I thought I'd give you a call. Are you glad?"

"Of course I'm glad. I just wasn't expecting one."

"So how are you?"

"I'm fine. A little while ago I decided to go shopping for fish, to make a fish dinner the way we both used to . . . no, Marianne, I'm not fine. I'm really not."

"Neither am I."

"Do you want to come back?"

"Do *you* want me to come back?"

"I don't know. Yes and no. Or—I don't know."

"That's exactly how I feel. It's still too early to tell, though. How's the place looking?"

"What sort of question is that? The place is looking the way it always looks. I haven't canceled the cleaning lady yet, if that's what you mean. What sort of stupid question is that?"

"Okay, let's leave it. It was just a question. Anyway, I think it's better if I stay at Olivia's for the time being."

"So that's what you think. And?"

"And what?"

"You must have some reason for calling me. Or was that it? You just wanted to ask if the place was clean? The place *is* clean. There must be something else."

"*Tho*mas."

"Sorry. My nerves are on edge, you know? I don't know what to do with myself.

"Are you applying for things? Are you looking for a new job?"

"Yes. That is, I'm planning on looking for one, but I've got too many other things on my plate at the moment."

"What sort of things?"

"I don't know. Just things. And anyway. Why are we talking about me? Why don't we talk about you? You're the one who moved out. When are you moving back in again?"

"I haven't moved out."

"You haven't? I must have missed something. It's funny, but I thought you'd been away for four weeks."

"You're right, but I haven't moved out, it's just—I think it's better if I stay at Olivia's for a few more weeks. And that's what you think, too, or you'd have called ages ago. I thought you'd have called."

"You thought. You tell me you're going to Olivia's for a week. I immediately think: she isn't going to come back after that week. And then she *doesn't* come back. Any normal person in my position would have called, I know that. But I didn't feel like calling."

"Weren't you afraid something might have happened to me?"

"Yes, I was. But Olivia would have been the first person to call me if something had happened to you. Since neither you nor Olivia called, I knew you were fine. Better than I was, at any rate."

"I'm sorry I didn't call."

"You just did."

"I've got a chance of a job here. Olivia has a friend who runs an advertising agency."

"Brilliant. That means you're going to get out of here."

"I don't know if I'm going to take it. Something in my life's got to change."

"Good idea. A divorce might be a good place to start. I don't get it!"

"Now hang on a minute."

"You want me to hang on? Four weeks—you could have been

dead for all I knew—and then you call to tell me you've got a new job, somewhere completely different, and you want me to hang on a minute? Do you want me to pack your things and send them to you? Is that why you're calling? Is that it? Yes? Well, *fuck it* is what I have to say to you, just fuck it."

"*Tho*mas."

"*Tho*mas, *Tho*mas, what's up, *Tho*mas!"

"I am coming back. Just not right now. That's what I wanted to tell you."

"You wanted to tell me that."

"Yes."

"And what if I didn't want you to? What if I were perfectly happy without you? What if that was how it was? Hm?"

"Then you'd have to tell me."

"Yes, I'd have to tell you. I'd have to tell you—and then everything would be fine, is that it? Like you're telling me now that you're coming home in a few months, or years, or whatever, is that it? Just a short call, darling. I'm not coming back just yet, and that's it?"

"No, it's not like that."

"It's exactly like that."

"Do you love me?"

The question is so sudden, it takes me so by surprise. It is uttered, it strikes me, with such disarming honesty, and yet such stupidity, that the best thing I can think of to do is to hang up. Fantastic. I've just answered Marianne's question about whether I love her by pressing the "on-off" button. That's not right, and I know it. I'll have to call her back. I'm sorry, I'll have to apologize. What am I to do, damn it? I look for Olivia's number and of course I can't find it. The phone rings. Marianne, it's Marianne.

"Hi, did you just put the phone down?"

"Of course I didn't, what gave you that idea? All of a sudden you weren't there and the line was dead."

"That's funny."

"Yes, I don't know, either."

"Thomas?"

"Yes?"

"I think we should be more honest with each other."

"That's what I think, too."

"I think what we both need more than anything else is time."

"Time to think, you mean."

"We've got to find out what we want, what our priorities are."

"Yes, of course, you're probably right."

"And then we can see how things work out for the two of us."

"Fine. So what'll we do now?"

"We'll call each other once in a while. I'll give you my number."

"I've got it, I've got it. It's Olivia's number, isn't it? I've got it."

"That's all we can do for the moment."

"You're right. You're probably right."

"I'm thinking about you, Thomas. And I hope we can work things out."

"Yes, I hope so, I'm thinking about you, too."

"Ciao."

"Ciao."

I hear her putting the phone down, the line going dead. I think to myself: that was me being sacked. My second sacking, so to speak. Two sackings a month, that's not a bad average. Let's see if I can keep it up. There are plenty of things I could be sacked from. My bank accounts, my credit cards, my flat, my TV connection—oh, there's no shortage of things. I'm not sixteen years old anymore, I'm not going to fall for that old "We need lots of time to think" nonsense. That's the classic line that the woman comes out with when she's planning to make a break for it. And I really don't have much thinking to do. My wife has made a break for it already. I walk back and forth in the apartment, talking to myself. Great. So that's how it is. My eye rests on my image in the wardrobe mirror. How do I look? I look at myself closely. I look as though I urgently need to go out.

25

'm about a foot and a half taller than usual. It's not a lot, but it's not to be sneezed at, either. If I force my jaws apart and laugh— I'm laughing a lot—I could swallow up this whole place, or at least the little blonde there in front of me, what's her name again? Anatol must have introduced her to me at least five times.

"What's your name again?"

She rolls her eyes irritably and Anatol comes to my aid: "She's still called Sabine. As she was ten minutes ago, the last time you asked."

My good mood doesn't seem particularly infectious. No one else has picked it up apart from Uwe, who isn't saying anything but has been grinning uninterruptedly for some time now. This is due to the fact that I've just done some coke with him in the men's room. I haven't done coke since my graduation party. I wonder whether my mother really did endure the torments of childbirth so that I could now find myself, at the age of thirty-five, coked up and unemployed, with people like Uwe, Anatol, and Sabine in a dive like the Funkadelic, unable to stop laughing. Was it really worth it? I mean, all the efforts of education, paying for my training, all that. The answer is, without a doubt: Yes, because I feel fantastic!

Marianne, who's responsible for the fact that I am spending my evening like this, must surely see that she isn't the only person in the world. I'm in it, too. And there are other women, like Sabine, for example. My problem at the moment lies in the fact that after all those Johnny Walkers and all that coke I'm not thinking too straight.

I don't think Anatol introduced Sabine to me for no reason at all. It's supposed to be some kind of a token from one man to another, because we're working together now. He's told me how he knows her, but I couldn't make it out because of the noise in here. The gestures that accompanied what he was saying also meant: If you're nice to this girl, you might get her into bed.

And being nice is exactly what I'm finding difficult. She really didn't like the fact that I forgot her name so quickly, and so many times in a row. Although that wasn't the plan. In the meantime I've switched to just smiling at her, and I've been doing that for quite a long time.

And lo and behold, success! Success! She leans over to me to tell me something, but unfortunately I can't hear her. There's all that stupid noise again. I smile sweetly at her and shrug my shoulders.

She repeats what she said, I still can't make it out. She turns away abruptly and talks to Anatol. He's evidently understood, walks over to me, and yells in my ear:

"Sabine wants to know if you'd mind not staring at her tits for five minutes."

Excuse me? That's not nice. I was smiling charmingly at her, that's all. I yell in Anatol's ear: "I wasn't staring at her tits. Tell her not to get ideas about herself."

Anatol gives a dismissive wave. I have to smile, too, although I really don't like the way things are going here. So I turn to Uwe, in whose tanned and peroxided head all the lights seem to have gone out. He's staring, mouth half open, at the dance floor, and nodding to the rhythm of the music. At a hundred and twenty beats a minute it looks like the final stages of Parkinson's. Prompted by the direction of Uwe's gaze, I walk over to the dance floor. None of my friends come with me. The music's so loud over there that it makes not only conversation impossible but even the most rudimentary thought. I have to stop walking because I've stumbled into a stroboscopic storm that makes it hard for me to put one foot in front of the other. I've come to a standstill by one of the tables at the edge of the dance floor. I try to make out other people as well as I can in this light. I could easily imagine bankers coming here to score. The crowd's a funny mixture of clubbers and fairly young members of the establishment. In my three-piece I must look like a bank employee on a drug-fueled break. That's exactly how I want it to look, because it's exactly what I am, a bank employee on a drug-fueled break, although for an unspecified period of time. Something in me, my sober self, perhaps, suddenly starts coming over all reasonable, and I'm thinking I've got to give my life direction again, and so on. What on earth am I doing here? Getting involved with coke dealers four weeks after being fired? How long will it be before I end up in the park in front of the bank, waving over at the entrance in the early morning: "Hi, guys, I've switched jobs. I've got a new career in drugs."

I'm not really worried about that, of course. But the fact is, I have no idea what to do. I haven't the faintest idea. Maybe I should start sending out résumés, as Marianne said. But for some peculiar reason I really, *really* don't feel like it. I don't know why, but I've just left that all behind me. Nothing like the Kosiek case—or should I say the Rumenich case—is going to happen to me twice. And I'm clearheaded enough to know that if I got a new job at a different bank, such things would be inevitable.

I don't know what to do, so I start dancing. Considering the state I'm in, that sounds easier than it is. I don't think I'm going to manage to stay with the beat for any length of time, and in any case, I haven't much strength left. I'm not in the best of shape. But there's life in me yet.

26

'm sitting with Uwe and Anatol in the Café Blue, trying to stay upright. Anatol says I've got to drink a Bloody Mary with loads of Tabasco—that would get me back in shape. I feel utterly wretched. To get him to leave me in peace I order myself one, three shakes of Tabasco, a good stir, take a sip, and then go off and throw up for a minute or two.

When I come back I find that Uwe and Anatol have started talking about the business that brought us all together in the first place. The prospect of dealing with something other than myself makes me feel better all at once.

They're talking about the man I've always called the Serb, the one who got out, the guy who persistently offered Marianne the use of his appliances. He's called Miro, and he's Anatol's brother-in-law.

"Now we're going to tell you how things get done," says Uwe. I must look surprised, because he adds by way of explanation: "Bellmann's on our tail. He called again yesterday. He'll be here again any minute. And you're going to help us get rid of him. For good."

"What do you mean by 'for good'?" I ask.

Uwe laughs. "Just that we want him to go away again."

Anatol and Uwe laugh loudly. It really is quite comical. They stop as abruptly as they started. Then we huddle a little closer together, and they explain to me "how things get done," with Uwe supplying what you might call the dramatic framing narrative, while Anatol fills in the occasional detail. It takes a long time and is made a lot more complicated than it needs to be. Presumably they're trying to impress me. They certainly manage to do that.

Uwe, competent and predestined to this particular task by his function as bodybuilder and fitness studio manager, is in charge of the illegal trade in bodybuilding preparations, most of them steroids, things like stearin, and he'll sell you coke but he doesn't consider that the actual purpose of his business. The cocaine is there because people want it. They buy steroids from him, and while they're buying one lot of illegal drugs, understandably enough, they figure they might as well get a little bag of coke at the same time. You're ranked as a dealer if you've got both. The steroid crowd aren't junkies, they just do coke to feel better when they're training. *Even* better, says Uwe.

Apart from that line of business, Uwe has the fitness studio, which more or less pays for itself. Anatol's Period Furniture Paradise is far more important here. Uwe tells me he wants to keep his books in order, so all the illegal money he makes with the steroids and the drugs gets laundered through Period Furniture Paradise. It's at this point that Miro gets involved. Anatol describes him as a responsible, trustworthy businessman who just ran into a few "difficulties," which is why he went back to Serbia. He's the one who ran up the debts at Furnituro Ltd. Miro uses a network of relations and acquaintances all around the world to make sure Anatol's orders keep coming in. Demanding customers in Ljubljana, Paris, Bucharest, Moscow, London, and New York are so impressed by Anatol's furniture that they want complete drawing rooms, dining rooms, and bedrooms. They need to decorate their whole houses. Miro makes sure only very big orders come in. Anatol accepts them all, issues bills of delivery, and invoices and confirms, with thanks, the payments that the customers have made. Of course no one ever gets any furniture delivered, and no one ever pays a bill. The bills are paid with Uwe's illegal earnings, which thus enter the books and emerge whiter than white. Not all of his illegal earnings—only what's necessary to keep Period Furniture Paradise on its feet as a business. In fact the assessors and the tax office consider Period Furniture Paradise a model business, and as far as the authorities are concerned, Anatol is very careful to stress that he has no links to Furnituro Ltd., from whom he bought the shop for one mark when Miro was broke.

The whole thing runs extremely smoothly. The only risk, the only awkward area, it seems to me, lies in the procuring of steroids and drugs. But Uwe says he's aware of that, and he's working with people who are one hundred percent reliable and nothing can go wrong. He's just worried about Bellmann.

Of course Bellmann also knows that Uwe and Anatol don't have any "official" connection with Furnituro Ltd., the only part of the business that owes any money to the bank. Nonetheless, he won't stop worrying about my two friends. So Uwe's suspicion that Bellmann might have discovered something about the collaboration between himself and Period Furniture Paradise isn't so unlikely. And it's at this point that I become useful to him.

A lot of things are running through my head right now. Uwe and Anatol, whom I used to think of as small-time traders whose business practices were perhaps not always as lily-white as they might have been, are revealing themselves to be committed, well-organized gangsters, with a respectable amount of criminal energy. And without understanding it, I've become their intimate accessory and accomplice. Given all that they've told me, I should really go the police and turn them in. But Uwe and Anatol have put me on their payroll, so I don't. And what reason would I have for ratting on them? You think if they break the law, a citizen like myself is obliged to report it immediately? You're right, of course—what my friends are doing is illegal. But that's the aspect of our collaboration that interests me the least. Quite honestly I can't see anything as being illegal where money is concerned. Everything revolves around the idea of advancing your own interests or the interests of whoever it is that's paying you. I can't see why it should be wrong to sell steroids to people who want to use them to make themselves more beautiful or kill themselves, while it isn't wrong for bourgeois lives to be ruined by exponential increases in a bank's interest rates. Excuse me, but I've never registered that kind of distinction; that's something for gullible people who claim it "means" something to them to live in a state with a legal basis, although they haven't the faintest notion what that basis might be.

We're talking about money, here, remember, and you know very well that only one law applies here: Do what thou wilt. Anyone who doesn't evade his taxes is an idiot. Anyone who gets caught doing it is even worse. You might see that differently; you might say your taxes are used to build schools, roads, kindergartens, old people's homes. But have you ever thought how that really happens— the construction of an old people's home, for example, *any* old people's home? A contractor hires an architect, a genuine idealist and friend of humankind, to plan an old people's home that would fill any old person's eyes with tears of joy. He gets good, solid craftsmen, who pay their Social Security contributions, to put forward terrifying bids for the construction costs, and when he's done that, he applies for state funding, *your* taxes, which he immediately gets ahold of. He has the old people's home built by moonlighters who live in the most awful poverty, and pays them two marks an hour but lets them sleep on the building site. With what's left over he buys himself an estate in Majorca with its own golf course and a plane to get him there faster. You read about cases like that in the paper every day. *Every* day. So give me an honest answer: Who's the idiot—the builder, who's done his job, or you, because you forgot to evade your taxes?

Anatol and Uwe have taken the wisest and most sensible path. They invest part of their illegal earnings to make their businesses look respectable, so they can go about their business unmolested. With the bulk of what's left over, they buy whatever they want: cars, women, houses . . . I enjoy Anatol and Uwe's stimulating and intelligent company.

27

Uwe evidently isn't quite sure, after all, that I'll keep my trap shut, and has pushed an envelope with thirty one-thousand mark notes over the table to me, the way my old uncle used to give me presents on Christmas Eve. Of course I couldn't see how much money there was in the envelope. I figured a few thousand, five at most, like last time.

Immediately after I came home I opened the envelope and counted it. Thirty thousand-mark notes. Thirty thousand is a ridiculously large amount for what I'm supposed to be doing. I've promised to have a word with Bellmann and convince him that Uwe and Anatol have nothing to do with Furnituro Ltd. That shouldn't be hard, because apart from a few minor suspicions, Bellmann has nothing to support his assumption, or else all hell would have broken loose long ago.

I don't understand why my new friends have drawn me into their confidence so easily and for no real reason, or why they're paying me so much. Have they overestimated my influence at the bank? Are they planning something I haven't guessed? Or are they chucking money around to impress me?

I sit at the kitchen table and shuffle the thirty thousand-mark notes like playing cards. There's a big difference between having your salary, for example your end-of-year bonus, which in my case was always the same amount, paid into your account by your employer, or like this, cash in hand, with no Social Security deductions or any of that crap. Not because it's cash but because it's criminal money, genuine and authentic criminal money. It comes straight out of the drawers of some drug-addicted bodybuilder who has presumably stolen it in the first place. The money feels like a shotgun, as forbidden, as immediately dangerous, as that. It cries out to be spent the way it came in: all at once, in a grand gesture.

I call Sabine, the bimbo my friends have been thrusting at me. Lest you misunderstand me: I'm not even slightly interested in her. Or rather, hang on, I am very interested in her, but not because I'm "in love" or whatever. So what should I do? Phone Marianne and suggest that we blow thirty thousand? She'd ask questions, she'd want to know where it came from, and so on. That wouldn't be so bad. I'd tell her. But then she wouldn't enjoy spending it with me. She'd say she no longer understood what I was up to anymore. I can't claim to understand what I'm up to myself. You'd think a man of my age, with my CV, my work experience, and so on, would have better things to do than hang out with criminals like Uwe and Anatol. But I don't care. I know exactly what would happen to me if I decided to return to my earlier career path. But I have no idea where my involvement with Uwe and Anatol will lead. That's the crucial, wonderful difference.

"Hello?"

She answers in a sleepy I'm-a-little-kitten voice. It's three in the afternoon.

"Thomas here."

"Hi."

She sounds really bored, meaning: if this conversation is to have a future, you're going to have to tell me something *very* exciting *very* soon. Well, I *have* something that should hold her attention.

"It's a lovely afternoon out there, Sabine. Time to get up and do something with it."

"I've got a hangover. Why are you calling me? Is something up?"

"No, nothing. I just wanted to know if you'd like to go shopping with me."

"Shopping? Brilliant idea. But I've got no money."

"Would I call you to tell you how to spend your money? I'm the one with the money. And I'm inviting you on a shopping spree."

I'm talking like Father Christmas.

"Sounds nice."

I can hear from the brighter tone of her voice all of a sudden that she hasn't got a hangover, she hasn't got a headache, and in a flash she's besotted with me—and wide awake. We've quickly arranged to meet in front of Dolce and Gabbana in the city's smartest shopping street.

I get myself ready, put on a black suit, choose a tie to go with it, and set off for the subway which, it dawns on me, used to be my way to work, but has now miraculously become my gateway to a completely different life.

I'm carrying the envelope with the thirty thousand marks in the inside pocket of my jacket. Going into business with Uwe and Anatol hasn't thrown me off course at all. I haven't done anything yet that could create problems for me. I've taken money, sure—but that isn't forbidden in itself. I've given promises that I might not be able to keep, for example, if—and I can't imagine this happening—I failed to convince Bellmann. Even then I could still pay them back and tell them I have no influence on Bellmann, and it would be as though nothing had happened. I could do that right now, then buy myself a newspaper and study the want ads. I could write off a bunch of applications and find another job over the next few months. Instead, though, I walk along the street that used to take me to work, to go shopping with Sabine, and once that's behind us, nothing will be the way it was before. This is going to be a shopping experience on an existential scale.

I'm feeling good. I want to go into a furrier's, but it turns out that Sabine hates fur. I'm always surprised these days that people like Sabine, who can't have had any kind of political education, reject the wearing of fur as incorrect. She repeats what she's heard

with pious intensity: animals kept in appalling conditions, endan-
gered species being exterminated, wearing fur amounting to en-
dorsing the murder of animals, and so on. I get so much of this that
my head spins, so I grip her by the wrist and drag her into Dolce
and Gabbana so we can get shopping as quickly as possible. A bit
uncertain at first, she starts taking out shoes and looking at the price
tags. Each time she finds that an item's been reduced, she tells me.
I tell her to ignore it. She laughs anxiously: "I always keep an eye
out for things marked down."

"So do typists. But you're not a typist. Are you a typist? Tell
me: Are you a typist?"

I'm amazed how worked up I've become.

"Look for things that have been marked up in price," I tell her.

"Nothing's been marked up."

"Who cares. Find yourself something decent, something expensive. Not the kind of crap that everyone has, but the things they'd
all *like* to have."

She gets nervous, I'm confusing her. She has a look at some
T-shirts—T-shirts!

"How much are they?"

"Two hundred and fifty each."

"Two hundred and fifty? Why take two? Take twenty!"

"I don't want twenty."

"Why not?"

"What am I going to do with twenty Dolce and Gabbana T-
shirts?"

"Wear them. Give them away. How should I know? Or find
something else."

For God's sake, why doesn't she just go for it? Her whole life
long, the slut hasn't had a thought in her birdbrain but: I want *that*
dress, I want *those* trousers, I want *that* blouse, I want *those* shoes,
I want *that* jacket, and so on and so on. Now, all of a sudden, it's
all hers for the asking, and she doesn't understand. I don't even want

to fuck her for it. As we entered the shop she asked me what I wanted from her. I said, "I don't want to fuck you. I want you to go shopping. Shopping in the grand style. And I want to watch you doing it."

And she simply won't get it, the silly bitch, when all I really want to do is throw away my money, my hard-earned money.

28

The shopping trip with Sabine was a disaster. When we were in Versace she managed to find a scarf, a silk scarf costing a whole four hundred and fifty marks. Before we went to Versace we'd been in Helmet Lang, Gucci, and Prada, and I still had twenty-five thousand in my pocket. I was getting really furious. I tried to explain to her that this wasn't exactly what I'd meant, and she burst into tears.

I bought her the stupid silk scarf, and she resisted and tried to tear it out of my hand when I went to the cashier, but I bought the thing and stuffed it into one of her shopping bags. She started getting really unpleasant when we went down, still arguing, to the subway station. So did I, though. She called me a "flash fucker" and I, rather unimaginatively, called her a "stupid cunt." Bystanders turned around to look at us because of the shouting, so I left Sabine standing on her own, howling, with five thousand marks' worth of clothes in her shopping bags, and it wasn't nearly enough.

I've decided to buy a car. A twenty-five-thousand-mark car really isn't anything special. I'm going to trade in our old Japanese heap—I'd be surprised if I got more than five thousand for it—and buy myself a Jaguar. The Jaguar Double Six is a nice car, and I should be able to get one secondhand for thirty thousand.

It's Saturday morning, and I set off, wearing my suit as usual, for the car showrooms.

The car showroom I go to is called Motorama and is, like every car showroom, a pitiful place. It's where lots of buyers experience their Day of Reckoning. They turn up with their savings, the credit they've squeezed out of their banks with false data, for "dream cars" palmed off on them by creeps with criminal records and sweaty armpits and a smile that tells you everything you need to know. While they're still counting the money, the dream car disintegrates on the way back from Motorama, the exhaust falls off, the gears give out, the alternator bursts into flames, and of course there's no chance of compensation. There is much wailing and gnashing of teeth: they should have known from the start, and they *did* know, but their desire for an Alfa Romeo Spider, a Corvette, a Ford Mustang, or even an Audi A3, a Ford Fiesta, or a Golf turbo-diesel was too powerful, too great, and the fulfillment of that desire promised to be happiness, simple happiness.

Of course no one at Motorama, buyers or salesmen, is so stupid that he doesn't know all this, or at least fear it. And even so, these people all play out the roles assigned to them—the salesmen with great relish, the buyers feeling like small animals on slaughtering day. The buyers exude their own limited dreams along with the sweat of their fear, and at the same time, fingering their wallets, they go on running their hands along various "models," as the salesman calls them. They're always slightly hunched, as though expecting a punch in the face. And while the salesmen tell them a pack of lies, they nod enthusiastically, although they're thinking, "No! No!," and then they pay in cash.

But I don't care about any of that. If they cheat me, if they pull a fast one, I don't care. I want a Jaguar Double Six for thirty thousand, and I really don't care if it'll still be on the road by next week.

Nonetheless, I stalk around the display cars like everyone else, when I notice a couple who are after something expensive, just like me. Because she's with a man, I don't immediately recognise Madame Farouche as Madame Farouche. That must be her husband, I think, as I watch her stand by a green Lexus making gestures that suggest she's weighing things up. Her physical posture, her hair color, and her hairdo, her face, as far as I can tell from a distance, leave no room for doubt—that certainly is Madame Farouche standing there, and yet it takes me a minute or two to register the fact. She acts as though she hasn't seen me—perhaps she actually hasn't.

I break out in a sweat, as though I've been caught red-handed. I don't want her to spot me, and decide to get out of Motorama as quickly as I can.

Is it coincidence, I wonder, that we should meet here?

Of course not. Employees from my bank get discounts at Motorama, and I came here in the hope that I might still be able to wangle something as an ex-employee.

Nonetheless, of course, I'm appalled to see her here. When I turn around, her eye briefly meets mine. She just happened to be looking up vaguely, and immediately recognized me. And she has seen that I have seen her, and it's too late. I have to go and say hello; I don't want to stand there like a complete loser.

"Madame Farouche! What a lovely coincidence!" I shout across the car roofs. A horribly tortured smile appears on her face, and this immediately lifts my spirits. Evidently the encounter isn't as frightful to her as it is to me, but I have the advantage of making the first move.

"This must be your husband. I'm sorry to say that I've never met you," I jabber once I've reached them. Monsieur Farouche slackly responds to my handshake and looks quizzically at his wife.

"What are you doing here?" asks Madame Farouche, almost enchantingly stupid with surprise.

"The same as everyone else. I'm buying a car!"

"Are you well?"

"What a question! I'm fantastically well!"

"That's nice," she says. It seems as though she's struggling to maintain her composure. We stand facing each other for several moments, in the course of which it becomes clear that we have nothing, absolutely nothing, nothing whatsoever to say to each other. So we chatter away.

"Herr Schwarz. This is Herr Schwarz, my boss. At the bank, until a few . . ."

"I've switched."

"I see."

"And now?"

"I'm self-employed."

"Interesting."

"That sounds great."

"So what are you doing? Consulting?"

"Yes, you might say that."

"That is the trend, increasingly."

"That's right."

"Hm."

"Very nice."

"Very nice to see you again."

"Yes, I saw you and thought, I must just . . ."

"Of course!"

"Why not?"

We tell each other to enjoy our shopping, but of course it's clear that we're all about to head for home. Who wants to be watched when he's buying a car? It's intimate, embarrassing, spending that amount of money. Is it really? Not for me. Not anymore. What I'd really like to do is slap down thirty brown thousand-mark notes on a car roof, right in front of Madame Farouche's eyes, and yell at a salesman: "I'm taking this one. Drive it out! And be quick about it!" But Madame Farouche and her husband have left Motorama so quickly after our meeting that no opportunity for such a display presents itself. I suddenly feel exhausted and confused, so I travel home the way I came—on the subway.

29

Bellmann has called and invited me to dinner at Lehmann's. The reason he gave was as dishonest as it was pitiful. "I just thought that I didn't want to break off contact as quickly as that. We've been colleagues for too long to act as if nothing had happened." Not a word about Uwe and Anatol. I wanted to tell him to his face that he was an asshole, but then I thought about the thirty thousand and kept my mouth shut.

Bellmann had reserved a table for two at the back of the restaurant, "so that we won't be disturbed," as he said jovially when I walked in. Because I know what he's up to, his simple and friendly smile strikes me as slimier than it perhaps is. I haven't been back to Lehmann's since I left the bank, and it takes me a minute or two to come to terms with that. The word FIRED is emblazoned on my forehead, and anyone who looks at me for so much as a moment can read it.

On the chef's recommendation we order buffalo wings and highballs. While we wait, Bellmann won't stop talking. His ceaseless chatter causes me physical pain, although it doesn't seem to bother him. Most likely he doesn't even notice. He tells me about his wife, who's finally pregnant after consulting a number of doctors to find out why the I.V.F. wasn't working. But now at last the time has come. I think he's expecting some kind of congratulations from me, but I don't say anything. When the good news reached them, his in-laws spontaneously decided to let their daughter have her inheritance early. Along with what Bellmann and his wife saved over the past few years, when they'd both been working, that would be enough, he explained, for a semidetached house in a suburb with a subway connection. They had some "brilliant design concepts" there—that's actually the expression he used. If you bought a semi just before it was built, you could even have a hand in deciding the distribution of the rooms and the nature of the floor, "absolutely custom-made," he exclaims excitedly. He tells me all this, I assume, to show me that he's climbed an extra rung up the social ladder, unlike me, the one who got sacked. The fact that I was always given preferential treatment in the bank must have been more of a thorn in his side than he let on. He concludes his tale about the suburban semi in a way that confirms this. He abruptly furrows his brow into caring folds and asks, "And how are *you?*"

"I bought a Jaguar Double Six yesterday," I lie.

"Oh, really. Madame Farouche said she saw you in Motorama. She said you didn't look happy."

The damned bitch! The snake!

"Yes, I was really unhappy to have run into *her.*"

We have a rather forced laugh together.

"And, um, how's your wife? Is she well?" Bellmann asks, changing the subject, or rather lumbering from one gaffe to the next.

"Marianne left me. She moved out. Sometimes we speak on the phone. Rarely. Very rarely."

"I'm . . . sorry about that."

"Oh, come on, you shouldn't let it get to you," I sneer.

"Is it—is it very bad for you?"

"You'll laugh," I say, very serious now, "it really isn't—*bad.* All in all, you could even say it's astonishing how little difference such a separation makes. As long as you avoid one another."

The waiter brings us our drinks. Bellmann lowers his forehead and pulls his glass toward him. Now, I see, he's going to get to the point.

"You were the one who passed on Furnituro Ltd. to me, so it can hardly surprise you that I'm still on the case," he begins.

I'm surprised at how agitated this introduction makes me. I really want to come out with everything all at once and say, "Uwe and Anatol have nothing to do with it," at which Bellmann would doubtless laugh himself sick, and rightly so. To calm myself down I take a sip of my highball, and its poison shoots straight to my brain.

"You remember we suspected that the new owners of this business might be the front men for the old one?"

Wrong, the old owners were the front men for the new one, I think to myself. But of course I'm not going to correct Bellmann's mistake.

I say, "Yes, we went for that theory at the time, but we had no clues, let alone proof. Have you got anything new on it?"

"You'll understand that I can't talk openly about that."

I look around for the waiter and answer, "Fine, that's that, then."

"Hang on, hang on. I *want* to involve you in this. I want you to help me. You live on the block where the owners of Furnituro have both their shops."

"So?"

"I thought—maybe you could make some kind of contact with the owners. Maybe you could find something out."

"Of course. But what's in it for me?"

I can't believe the way things are going. He's about to offer me more money.

"I can promise that I'll put in a word for you with Rumenich."

"Are you joking? I don't want to work at your lousy place again. I'm working on my own now, do you understand? You can ask Rumenich how much money she's going to put on the table. Then we can talk."

"I've already asked her."

"You're on the ball, Bellmann!"

"She says she'll up your severance by thirty thousand if you're willing to play."

"And what do I have to do for that?"

"Get to know the guys who run Period Furniture Paradise and

Ladies Only. Find out what they have to do with Furnituro Ltd. Write a confidential report about it and give it to me. And the check'll be yours."

"Isn't that an awful lot of work for thirty thousand? And what if the guys turn out to have nothing to do with Furnituro?"

"If your report's convincing, you get the money, whatever happens."

Bellmann is right. There isn't the slightest reason to reject the offer. After some more dithering, I agree. After that I feel a bit more at ease. Only when we leave Lehmann's, and he walks me to the subway and starts on about his semi again, do I really feel like punching him. When we say goodbye I give him such a firm handshake that he pulls a rather startled face. But he doesn't say anything. Bellmann has never said anything whenever I've hurt him in the past. As I walk down the escalator I can just see him tumbling down the steel steps, breaking his teeth and cutting himself quite badly. If the opportunity presented itself, I think, Uwe would beat somebody like Bellmann to a pulp, and at the moment that doesn't seem such an awful way of achieving internal equilibrium. Not my style, though, sadly.

30

nactive days spent dully and alone in my apartment. My sole source of food is Dial-A-Pizza. I alternate between calzone and Hawaiian, washed down with Coke. Enormous quantities of Coke to stay awake and alert, but it doesn't work. An inexpressible sense of grief has brought my brain to a standstill. It's inexpressible because I don't know what I'm grieving for. My marriage? My job? My mental health? A wonderful phrase, "mental health." What does it mean? Do I have such a thing? I sit at the living room table and play patience with the Coke bottle tops. I could go to the supermarket and buy food, cook something fantastic, a banquet all for me, and get myself drunk on a bottle of Cabernet Sauvignon. Our supermarket is sensational; they've got everything, they've got more than everything. More than anyone could possibly be familiar with. But it's ten minutes away, on foot. The way I feel, a ten-minute march on foot would be like a death sentence.

The sight of the things in my place numbs me. It has nothing to do with the fact that they remind me of Marianne, it's because nothing here has changed, and that in turn is because I've got a cleaning lady who comes once a week. How am I supposed to have any realistic sense of my decline, my self-neglect—because that's what it is—if my surroundings don't change at all?

Salvation comes, as it does so often in my life, from the telephone.

"Uwe here. Things are getting serious now."

"What? What's getting serious?"

"Bellmann's here. With a bailiff. He's got a search warrant. I'd say it's time for you to get down here."

"Down where?"

"Down to the fitness studio! They're not going to wait for much longer. Get down here!"

He hangs up. I'm completely out of shape, but I leap into a suit as quickly as I can and run down to Ladies Only.

Bellmann's standing there with Schmidt, Bailiff Schmidt of all people, who's sniffing around a tanning bed, which he presumably wants to impound. Uwe and Anatol stand motionless but visibly furious at the reception desk. Uwe drums his fingers on the tabletop.

Bellmann sees me coming and yells angrily, "Hi, Thomas. Not the best possible moment."

Uwe thumps his fist on the bar and yells at Bellmann, "This is our adviser!" Then Bellmann, Uwe, and I all talk at the same time.

"Just one moment. This is my former colleague from the bank."

"I know very well who I'm working for. Bellmann, I've got to talk to you."

"What are you going on about?"

"You had a job to do!"

"What? You were the one with the job to do!"

"I was not!"

"That's a lie!"

And so on. Finally I grab Bellmann by the sleeve and pull him into the corner of the studio, over by the sauna. I whisper furiously at him, "Bellmann! Don't act more stupid than you are! Of course I'm not here by chance. I managed to win these guys' trust. I acted the embittered, unemployed banker out for revenge. They tell me everything, do you understand? And then you turn up with that piss artist Schmidt and ruin it all. Are you crazy?"

Bellmann clutches his head in both hands. I interpret this as an attempt to think, and leave him alone for a few seconds before continuing.

"If you start waving your dick around here and impound everything you can think of, stuff you're going to have to give back within two weeks because it doesn't belong to Furnituro, you'll never learn who's involved with who. Give me a few weeks and I'll find out everything you want to know."

"You think they'll tell me if they've got anything to do with Furnituro? Why should they do that?"

"Because I'll tell them I can only work for them if I know who's in with who. I'll promise to keep the bank off their backs."

"You're a genius, Schwarz. But what's the guarantee that you aren't lying, and that you really aren't the embittered, unemployed banker who's out for revenge?"

"Bellmann! You're never going to make an enforcer! Think for a second! You have no choice. If you don't believe me, cart out everything that's in here and then bring it back in two weeks' time. These two guys are going to laugh at you. Not to mention Rumenich. She'll laugh at you, she'll chuck you out. But if you just let me get on with it, at least you'll have a chance to learn some stuff that will really get you ahead. Don't forget, I'm getting thirty thousand. That's a lot of money for me. I'm not going to let you down."

Bellmann slowly lowers his hands.

"Okay then. I'm depending on you, Schwarz. I haven't got a good feeling about it, but I can't think of anything better at the moment."

We walk over to Uwe and Anatol. I stand next to them and intone, "We understand each other. The whole business is based on a regrettable oversight. Herr Bellmann here was sitting on some false information. He's going to leave everything here exactly as it is and go back to his work with Herr Schmidt."

That's exactly what happens. Bellmann and Schmidt say goodbye, almost inaudibly, and disappear. Uwe and Anatol stay motionlessly where they are and look after the others in astonishment. When the door clicks shut, they burst out laughing. They roar with laughter. They slap me on the shoulders and ask me how I managed it. I grin, and say only, "Very simple. I made it clear to the guy that he had nothing on you."

"You seem to be worth your money, pal," says Uwe, suddenly rather reflective.

I reply, "Don't give it another thought. They're gone for now. But not forever, of course. They'll be back in a few weeks. Until then we've got to come up with a plausible idea about why you *couldn't* have anything to do with Furnituro Ltd. I'm sure something will come to me—for a reasonable sum."

31

I knew from the start that you'd come up with the goods," says Uwe, taking a pinch of coke on the tip of his little finger and rubbing it into his gums as though brushing his teeth. Then he rinses his mouth with a glass of prosecco. He's very pleased with himself, and with me. I'm very pleased, too. Still, I'm getting paid handsomely, twice, without really cheating anybody. No one's ever going to find out that I'm telling Bellmann an untruth. And in any case he's the only one interested in Furnituro Ltd. He doesn't understand that he could leave things just as they are and devote himself to other, more career-enhancing matters. But he thinks he has to present Rumenich with Uwe and Anatol's heads on a silver platter, so that he can say, "Oh, by the way, I've also taken care of that little unfinished problem that Schwarz left us with." Bellmann's chief concern is to establish common ground with Rumenich against me, and in actual fact the Furnituro business would be ideally suited to that—if I hadn't taken it upon myself to do Bellmann a bit of damage.

I don't need revenge. I'm just doing it for the money. Anatol takes the bottle out of his ice bucket and refills our glasses. Uwe has taken us to a tapas bar, he knows the owner, a German who seems to have had some success with property speculation in Andalusia. This man's a pretty repellent-looking character, with the sleeves of his jacket rolled up, "fashionable" three-day stubble, gold chain, and so on. He comes over to our table to say hello to Uwe. Uwe demands that I sit down next to him, and puts his arm around him. "This man here"—he points to me—"can be fully recommended if you have any problems with your bank."

"Which I always do."

"Fantastic."

Uwe is putting on a show, as if I'd done things like this for him before. But he's probably as serious about it as he seems to be. I don't believe that I'm as important to him, objectively speaking, as he may have assumed. But that isn't the crucial thing. What he wants to buy from me is my seriousness. You laugh? I *am* serious! My presence reassures Uwe. Criminals, even small-time ones like Uwe, need a good memory. They have to have all their lies and excuses at their fingertips, they have to think in eight directions at the same time. That can get tiring, and then it's nice to have somebody who's completely dependable. And I *am* completely dependable.

Sabine comes into the pub, and the moment I see her I break out into a cold sweat. My hope that she's here by chance, and not for our sake, shatters immediately. With a practically beaming smile, the first I've ever seen on her face, she marches up to our table—up to me! She hurls her arms around me, kisses me on the lips, and sits down beside me. I haven't a clue what she's up to, and give Uwe a quizzical look. He gestures to me to keep my mouth shut, it's all *fine*.

So not a word about our shopping trip, not a word about our argument on the subway. Uwe has—and I can guess how—relaunched project Sabine. I knew she was a slut.

Uwe and Anatol want to reward me, they crack jokes about my potency and ask Sabine if she doesn't want to check it out. It's utterly revolting, but I laugh along. I find it revolting and funny at the same time. Uwe's coke hasn't exactly dampened my spirits, either. I get drunk and start having a bit of a grope with Sabine, who doesn't resist.

She's wearing a tight red brocade dress, through which I can feel the outlines of her bra. With my arm around her, I fumble half discreetly about and try to keep a conversation going with Uwe and Anatol at the same time. We keep on talking the same crap, about how brilliant it was of me and how important I am for them, and how well it's all going to work, and so on. While we're talking, Sabine grabs my crotch under the table. She does it with the businesslike manner of a general practitioner, but that doesn't bother me.

Uwe says, "When this business has successfully run its course, there are a few other activities I'd like you to get involved in—if you like."

I'm a little distracted.

"Other activities?"

"Other activities."

"What kind?"

"Let's not talk about that here. Not now. I want you to meet a few of my clients."

"That sounds good. To our continued partnership."

We clink glasses, for the five hundredth time, to our imaginary partnership. Anatol refills the glasses again. Uwe takes a snort. Sabine discreetly kneads my balls. She doesn't do it in an uncontrolled and painful fashion, but just as though she wants to remind me about something.

She asks me if I'd like to invite her back to my place "for a coffee." I laugh and nod and wonder: Is that what people say? "For a coffee"? Why don't they say, "For a fuck"? Would that be less romantic? I'm not used to dealing with prostitutes. I've been to a brothel, of course, but that's a bit different; there's an atmosphere of secrecy there—at least in the corridors. I've never sat next to a slut in a bar, let alone one who's kneading my balls. Okay, Sabine isn't your whore off the streets—more what you would call an escort, or whatever. Or maybe only a part-time hooker who happens to be a friend of Uwe's, and who likes to earn a little on the side from time to time.

Whatever, we leave. Uwe and Anatol say goodbye to each other with plenty of winks and backslapping. Sabine and I take a taxi to my place.

We start making out wildly on the backseat of the taxi. She

tastes good, she smells good, so how come I don't really fancy her? The truth is: All I can think about is, how much is she getting for this? How much has Uwe paid her? How did they work it out? "One fuck for five hundred?" Or is it more like buying a car, when you discuss what comes as standard and what's extra? I push my hand between her legs, and she opens them as though to say, "Please, be my guest." So that seems to be included in the price. It starts getting too much for the taxi driver, who's been watching us all the time in his rearview mirror, and he sniggers, "Haven't you got a bed at home?" I withdraw my hand and say irritably, "You should keep your eye on the road." It seems he doesn't want a fight, and he shuts up. Fine. I even give him a tip when we get out. Sabine pulls her dress down for decency's sake, and we walk arm in arm to the front door, like a real pair of lovers.

32

I t's no damn use! I can't get a hard-on, for Christ's sake. What kind of stupid idea was it to go back to my place? Here in the apartment, everything's full of Marianne. I hadn't even thought of that, interestingly enough, when Sabine asked if we were going to my place. Couldn't I have thought of something better? Wasn't a hotel room included in the deal? I stand in indirect half-light, which is actually very atmospheric, with a half-erection, Sabine on her knees in front of me doing the best she can with it, as I squint up at the ceiling. No damn use at all.

Sabine seems to understand—or perhaps she doesn't. At any rate she lets go of my cock, stands up, and starts undressing. She performs one of those absurd little garter-belt dances that you see on TV shows at eleven o'clock in the evening. It's supposed to be seductive. I need help. I sit down on the edge of the bed.

"Please, Sabine, just leave it. Please stop."

She goes on, but with a bit less enthusiasm.

"What's wrong? Don't you like it?"

"Would I ask you to stop if I liked it?" I shout.

Insulted, she puts her dress back on and sits down on the edge of the bed, too, but three feet away. I look for my cigarettes, offer Sabine one, and we smoke. I feel like a gargoyle, sitting here in the half-light and smoking, silent and naked, with my lonely balls on the hard edge of my marriage bed, next to a strange woman whom I don't really want anything to do with.

"How much did Uwe pay you?" I ask coarsely.

"What for?"

"For this!"

"That's a completely unnecessary question, darling."

I look at her in astonishment. I've never heard her come out with anything like that, nothing so resolute. Is she classier than I imagine?

"What do you mean *unnecessary*? What's unnecessary?"

"Listen." Her voice starts getting all maternal. "I think we could really have some fun with each other if you'd only relax. I thought to myself, he's so cool! He lies down with another woman in his marriage bed. But apparently you're not so cool after all. I really don't care, we could go to a hotel—if you'd get some clothes on first."

What's the little slut thinking about? She's laughing at me! I say, "Okay, get your clothes off."

She scrutinizes me for a moment, then starts to undress. I jump into the wardrobe and get the envelope with the thousand-mark notes out of the inside pocket of my jacket. Sex and money must be connected in some way or another, I reflect vaguely. It can't be all that hard; it happens in every other sex film you see on TV—people fucking *in* money, I mean.

"Let's do something with the money," I say.

"Do you want to go shopping again? At this time of night?"

"No—something . . . dirty!"

She laughs. She laughs long and loud.

"Sorry, love, but if you want something dirty you're going to need more than a few thousand . . ."

"You think so? I don't. I mean, just think about the following: I'm a banker who's just been fired, and who has no fixed income. You are—let me guess—someone in medicine or technology who makes a bit on the side. And here we've got 'a few thousand,' as you put it—twenty-five thousand, to be precise—which is quite a lot."

"I don't mean its value. Or perhaps I do. No, I do mean its

value. Twenty-five thousand means a few months off, an exotic holiday, some nice furniture, clothes, whatever . . . but it's not *real* money."

"Of course. It isn't. But it's enough for us to *pretend* it was real money."

"Sorry, but games like that bore me."

"Hm, yeah, I admit it, they bore me, too."

I sit there again, at a loss and unable to understand why we aren't having a good time. I mean, what's going on here? Two reasonably young, reasonably attractive people in a bedroom, the money's taken care of . . . I ask her, "So what would you think of as real money?"

"I don't know. One, two, three million? Less? More? I couldn't say really. Much more important than the amount is whether it makes you *rich*."

"Rich?"

"Free."

"Oh of course. Free."

"Yes, free."

"And with twenty-five thousand? Could that make you free?"

"Yes, but only for a short time. So short that it wouldn't count."

I wait for a while. Then I say, "Okay then! Get your clothes on!"

I get dressed, too.

"What are you planning?"

I fetch the phone and call a taxi. Then I call the Holiday Inn and reserve a double room with a bath.

It takes us fifteen minutes to get there. We don't say a word. I pay the taxi driver, and Sabine waits until I get out and open the door for her. We walk through the automatic glass door and into the lobby. Although it's half-past two in the morning, the lobby is full of people. I get the keys and ask if I can pay immediately. They say that's fine, so I pay.

"I want to be able to clear out the minute I feel like it," I say to Sabine as we're going to the elevator.

"You can do that if you pay afterward," she answers.

"But this way I can simply run out of the building, or jump out of the window, and it's all taken care of."

"You're not very imcompulsive, Thomas, are you?"

We find the room we've reserved and walk in. I say to Sabine, "Okay, get your clothes off!"

We laugh. She comes over to me and we kiss. I run my hands over her body as though it were an object I'd just bought, whose purpose was not yet quite clear, which was still to be tested to see whether it worked well enough or not. Coolly and skillfully, she pulls down my trousers and starts kneading my cock. This time it works. We lie down on the bed and stroke each other, our lust rising until we're desperate to fuck, which is what we do. It takes about ten minutes. I find it incredibly exhausting. But on the other hand it's nice that Sabine should be so professional about the whole business.

When we've finished, our bodies lie naked, side by side, on the hotel bed. I'm not tired or exhausted in the slightest. I'm calm, because I know I've got a few very interesting hours ahead of me. I say to Sabine, "I want to fuck you until I can't anymore. That's what Uwe paid for."

Sabine smiles and says, "If you put another thousand on that, I'll show you a few things you *don't* know."

I wait for a minute, then stand up and walk over to my jacket. I take out a thousand-mark note and hand it to her.

"It'd better be worth it."

"You'll soon find out."

33

Well, it wasn't worth it, of course. Or maybe it was. Or not. Bored, I play around with the possible answers to this question as I sit at home alone in bed, sipping a cocktail of vitamin and magnesium tablets topped off by two aspirin with added vitamin C. Of course it's a very good thing that nothing actually happened with Sabine in this bedroom, in this bed. Marianne's stuff is all over the place here, she still lives here, but for weeks I haven't been able to imagine our marriage going on as before. And neither can she. Of course I've had a terribly bad conscience since last night. But why should I? She's the one who walked out. And there's still the tacit rule that nothing should change about our status as a couple for the time being, if only—for a while at least—to spare us the unpleasantness of separation. Obviously our cease-fire would break down the minute we had to get rid of our last shared things, selling our place and canceling our bank accounts. Of course our marriage would be one of those that are destroyed for good in an appalling battle over crockery, cutlery, furniture, and a few thousand marks. And perhaps, just perhaps, there's something else, too. I should call Marianne. But not right now. Not after the night I've had. Maybe in a few days. I haven't thought about her being away for ages, and I'm only thinking about it now because I've cheated on her. And how! I'll call her sometime soon.

And what about Sabine? I couldn't care less. I really don't care about her, quite honestly. That's exactly what makes her presence in my life so pleasant. I can order her up like a pizza. It costs a bit of money, but it doesn't give her the right to make demands. I could send her away whenever I felt like it, and it would be as though she'd never been there. Strictly speaking, it's a very comfortable state, and nothing for me to get terribly worked up about. What does my book *It's a Lovely Day Today* have to say on the subject? "Go your own way. Everything has been prepared. Your goal is uncertain. Joyfully accept everything that happens to you. It's all part of your personal life." That's it, right? All part of my personal life. I can't imagine the emotional range of the guy who wrote that.

Later that day I get dressed and go down to see my old pals in Period Furniture Paradise. I walk in through the shop door, ding-dong, and go to the office at the back. Uwe's there on his own. He looks unexpectedly serious. Slender half-moon spectacles, far too delicate for his fleshy head, sit on his nose, which he is holding bent over a stack of faxes on his desk. He lifts his head. When he sees me he smiles blandly.

"Well, did you have a good night?"

I think he expects me to thank him. I find it embarrassing, but what else can I do?

"Yeah, it was great, thanks."

He notices that I'm a bit ashamed of myself, and laughs at me for a moment or two. I laugh, too. Then he gets serious again. After a brief pause he says with a frown, "Listen up. I've got a good deal going. I've landed us a doctor from the National Olympic Committee, who's been fired. He's going to be able to get me a first-class delivery of steroids. It's coming from the States. The samples I've had were so good that I'm going to go ahead."

"That's nice for you. So what's the problem? And what can I do?"

"The problem is that we haven't got a safe place for the hand-over. And that's where you can help us."

"By doing what?"

"Organizing a safe place for us."

"A safe place. I can't think of anything off the top of my head. Apart from—"

"Apart from your apartment. Right?"

It isn't right, and I'm not exactly bowled over by the idea of Anatol, Uwe, a doctor for Olympic athletes and who knows what kind of thugs coming into my apartment to do their deals.

"Do you think that's a good idea? My apartment?"

"It's a *very* good idea. We'll arrange to meet our little friends here in the street, receive them in the fitness studio, and then we'll bring them blindfolded to your flat. We'll arrange your living room in such a way that they won't be able to identify any features. Then we'll get our goods, and they'll get their money. We'll blindfold them again and bring them down to the street. That's all."

"Isn't that—no disrespect, Uwe—a bit of a crap plan?"

"I don't give a shit if the plan's crap. The doctor's agreed to it. He's new to the business, and he's terrified of being discovered. So I suggested this to him—and he agreed."

"Sorry, but I think it sounds like a joke."

"No joke, Schwarz. This deal will get me goods worth two million for a knock-down three hundred thousand. I'm happy to give it some gangster talk if the clients find that reassuring."

"It's a rotten idea, Uwe."

"You've had thirty thousand marks from me, Schwarz."

"But not for this."

"For this, too."

"It's not enough."

"And there'll be more. You'll get another ten thousand."

"Sorry, Uwe, but it's not on. I'm not doing something like this for ten thousand."

From one second to the next Uwe's face turns scarlet, he leaps up at me from his desk like a wrestler and grabs me by the throat with both hands. He doesn't just press a little bit, he puts all his strength into it. I start panicking and try to twist his fingers back, but he has a grip like a monkey wrench.

"Listen, pal. You're a little asshole who I've given some money to make him work for me. Not to have a debate with him. I discussed the handover with the doctor, and that's how we're going to do it. Do you think I'm going to ring him up again and tell him we've had a complete change of plan? You're nuts!"

He shakes my throat like a sapling, then lets me go. I gurgle, choke, gasp for air. He goes back behind his desk and yells, "I'm not a monster. You, you bastard, get thirty thousand, and then we do it. Okay?"

For some reason I suddenly get a nosebleed. A real torrent of blood shoots out of my nostrils. Uwe shrieks, "Mind the carpet, you filthy fucker!"

He leaps at me with a brightly colored scrap of material that he got somewhere. I automatically flinch while he presses the scrunched-up rag to my nose and says, "Hold it there!"

So that's what my new job looks like. Am I wrong, or have I lost control of things once and for all? I wheeze, "Thirty thousand, you say? Thirty thousand is different. Ten thousand's nothing. Thirty thousand's okay."

"Of course thirty thousand's okay, man, I know that myself. Now fuck off."

I go up to my apartment and lie back down in bed. After a while my nosebleed stops. I look at myself in the mirror. I've got strangulation marks on my throat, and my nose is a bit swollen. There are scabs under my nostrils. I have a headache, so I lie down on the sofa in the living room. Everything in here is going to have to be cleared away, I think. And I feel sorry for myself.

34

I have—after such a long time!—finally arranged to see Markus at the Caravaggio again. I haven't been there since our last meeting.

"Hey, Thomas, since when have you been wearing cravats?" he calls coyly when I come in and sit down at our table, the same one as ever.

"Since I've had strangulation marks on my throat," I reply.

Markus is in a great mood and laughs so loudly that other customers turn around to look at us.

"I'm not joking, Markus," I say quietly, and pull my cravat down a little. He immediately stops laughing, and I pull it back up.

"Those aren't love bites, are they?"

"Markus. They're strangulation marks, finger marks. Somebody's been"—and I have to laugh myself—"putting pressure on me."

Markus laughs again, loudly. Once our laughter has subsided, he says, seriously, "So tell me what's going on."

"I've got some pretty serious shit hanging over me."

Laughter again, but not so loud this time.

"Seriously, I'm in big trouble."

"Why did you never call?"

"You never have time."

"Am I sitting here, or am I not sitting here? Fire away!"

"You know I'm not with the bank anymore."

"And now you've had two job offers and don't know which one to accept?"

"Absolutely not. I've done what they call falling into bad company."

"They can't be much worse than the people you were with at the bank, can they?"

"That's what I thought at first. At first I thought I had everything under control, but since yesterday I've realized that I haven't got anything under control. They have *me* under control. That's why I called you. You've got to help me."

"I'd love to help you if I can. Who are 'they'?"

"I can't tell you that. I mean—just answer one question: Is three hundred thousand marks a lot of money?"

"I don't know what you're talking about. Of course three hundred thousand is a lot of money. What did you expect me to say?"

I really can't let Markus in on what's happening. I decide to give the conversation a different spin.

"Oh, it's all half-baked stuff. I shouldn't have mentioned it. I'll find some kind of a solution. You know, since Marianne's been away . . ."

"Ah yes, Marianne. So she hasn't come back?"

Markus, thank God, doesn't linger over the three hundred thousand, even if he's now looking a bit confused.

"No, and I don't think she's going to."

"Is that what you want?"

"Let's just put it this way: the question doesn't bother me particularly. I don't miss her especially. We aren't officially separated. She's at her aunt's. Things are only going to get difficult if she wants a divorce, or if she wants to come back. I just don't want to have to do anything, like hiring a lawyer to deal with our divorce. That would be awful. Not because of the divorce as such, but because of all the hassle it would entail."

"Same here. I've reached an arrangement with Babs. We phone, it's nice. Sometimes we go and eat together, but nothing more than that. No sex, no passion. Feelings are nothing but trouble, don't you agree?"

"And what about the other woman? The one you were so hot for?"

"Oh, that's all over. I haven't seen her for two months. It just sort of ran its course. A lot of arguments, a lot of hassle. Feelings are trouble. I'm just not interested anymore."

"Then we agree."

We spend a few minutes attending to our cigarettes: taking them out of their packets, sticking them in our mouths, lighting up, smoking. Markus exhales smoke and asks, "But listen, what are you worried about if you've got three hundred thousand coming in?"

"I'm not worried. It's just that it isn't enough."

"What do you have to do for it?"

"I don't really know, exactly."

"I'd do anything for three hundred thousand."

I think about what to reply. I say, "Three hundred thousand is nothing, old pal. Three hundred thousand is shit. Five million, now you're talking. That's proper money. Ten million's too much."

"What in God's name are you *talking* about?"

"I've met this chick. Pert tits, good firm ass. She's called Sabine, she's dumb as pigshit. But she does what I tell her to because I pay her for it."

"Aha."

"What do you mean 'aha'? For the time being, at least, it's more convenient than worrying about woman trouble."

"Your woman trouble must be pretty intense if that's your way out of it."

"It is. So one more time: Is three hundred thousand a lot of money?"

"Not if you've got to leave the country. Not if you can never show your face again. Not if you have to . . . give up your whole identity."

"Okay," I say, "that is another way of looking at it."

We order lunch. The waiter recommends the fresh lobster. We

agree. Lobster and a bottle of Lacryma Christi del Vesuvio bianco 1993, please.

"You'll figure out the best thing to do."

"Believe it or not: what you've said has been a lot of help."

"What have I said?"

"That stuff about identity."

"Good, I'm glad. I said I'd be happy to help you if I could. So I've helped you. Now I have to ask whether you'd be willing to help me, too."

I should have seen that one coming. He's exploiting what I've said, of course he is. But I had to do it. I quickly decide not to go beyond a certain sum, and settle on ten thousand.

"I've got to fly to Manila with Babs, she wants to make a documentary about some lizards that are supposed to live there, and I'm going with her and afterward we're going to take a holiday."

"Manila."

"You've no idea what a flight to Manila costs. Of course you can't fly economy, it would finish you off."

"Please stop right there. If I remember correctly, you owe me around forty thousand."

"And you owe me a favor. You said so yourself."

"So what do you want from me?"

"Let's call the forty fifty. I'm working on a screenplay for a promotional film about the airport. Fee of sixty thousand. That gives us a bit of leeway. I get the money in three months, when I've finished. Then I'll transfer your fifty thousand over to you."

"Yeah, if that's how it is, I'd be *crazy* not to lend you money. It sounds like a really terrific deal for me."

He doesn't pay the slightest attention to my sarcasm. He raises his glass to me. I raise mine and say, "My dear friend Markus, you have no idea just what a help you've been, so how about I give you not ten thousand, but twenty? And because you've cheered me up so much with what you said, you don't have to pay it back."

Markus sits completely still for what feels like a long time. Then he takes a deep swig from his glass, puts it down, and says, "I don't know what to say, Thomas, but I think you're really fantastic."

"I'm glad, my old pal. I think I'm pretty fantastic, too. And so are you."

35

As though I've got a good fairy looking after me, I set off at the crack of dawn, fresh as a daisy, well dressed and fully packed, to the station, to go and see Marianne.

She phoned and invited me. Simple as that. She said, "Come and see me and Olivia, we'd love to see you. Olivia's giving a party." That *is* new, I thought to myself, and accepted. Seriously, what with the fact that that this invitation came out of the blue, no if's or but's, no conditions, no red tape, with none of the usual bullshit. I found it all actually quite liberating. So my step as I walk to the taxi is light and springy, and after he's brought me to the station safely and at an agreeable speed, the taxi driver gets a decent tip, for which he is suitably grateful.

No intruder is squatting in the first-class seat reserved for me, as has happened on several occasions in the past, and I set off in an almost festive mood, with a club sandwich, a fresh coffee, a glass of champagne, and a copy of the *Frankfurter Allgemeine Zeitung*. The friendly railway staff bring me all of these things in response to the tiniest gestures, and my every wish is catered to. Which is as it should be.

I am still wearing cravats, because the finger marks that Uwe left on my neck are still visible after a week. I'm a bit worried about what Marianne will have to say about that—and I don't know what I'll reply.

Marianne picks me up at the station in Olivia's car, a silver Audi TT. We greet each other with an almost shy little kiss, and spend the journey to Olivia's house chatting inconsequentially in a way that is supposed to be—at least this is how I see it—superficial and charming. For the duration of my stay here, I could tell from the tone of Marianne's phone call, peace on earth should prevail, and we are supposed to take time to find out whether we should "give it another try."

Of course the idea is completely and utterly doomed from the start, yet Marianne is delightedly going along with it it, because it's been suggested to her by Olivia, whom she considers to be worldly wise. So I've been forced to play along just to save face, although, as I've said, it's clear as day that nothing will come of it.

Olivia's husband, the oral surgeon, has bought himself and his family a plot on an idyllic wooded lake, and commissioned one of Frankfurt's star architects to build him a house that ridicules the very notion of the "one-family house." Some details: on the first floor—the first floor—there's a hundred-square-meter swimming pool, and above it a starry sky can be summoned by means of the most up-to-date electronics, a match for any planetarium. There are two wine cellars, one for the red wine, another for the white. Both wine cellars are about the same size as our apartment, and they are equipped with computer-regulated air-conditioning that compensates for any temperature variation of more than an eighth of a degree. Two technicians are employed to take care of the air-conditioning and lighting throughout the house, and they spend the whole day in a furnace room that looks like the control module in a space station.

Olivia welcomes us into her enormous French-designed kitchen. Her greeting seems cordial at first, but I must be gawking, because I prompt the remark, "Wealth is pleasant, but one should not overestimate its importance, Thomas."

I'm baffled by this observation. What's she thinking about? What has Marianne been telling her?

I say, "King Midas himself would have been happy with a palace like this. The sight of it depresses me every time I step inside."

Olivia laughs lightly, as though I'd said something quite different, as though I'd just paid her a little compliment. I can't over-estimate the importance of wealth, I think to myself, if I consider the relaxed, even polite impertinence with which Olivia ignores what I say. Whatever. Marianne and I are guided, with an appro-priate gesture, into a kind of drawing room furnished with a Bied-ermeyer suite that contrasts agreeably with the long-fiber orange carpet and the original Warhols on the walls. If Anatol and Uwe were actually to *sell* period furniture, they'd find a ready market right here. They don't, though. We sit down on a long white sofa, and a member of the domestic staff, actually wearing something like a uniform, brings us an aperitif, which Olivia has prepared for us in the kitchen.

The guests will be arriving soon, Marianne tells me. It's time to resolve the question of who's spending the night where, and we go upstairs. In *the same* room? Of course in *the same* room. It's all been made ready for us. My luggage, which I left at the front door, has been spirited upstairs by invisible staff.

"I'm glad you've come."

Marianne's expression contradicts her words. Her face isn't pleased, it's weak, resigned.

"Did things work out with the new advertising agency?" I ask.

"I was there for three days. Then I stopped going in."

I look at the floor in embarrassment. She's clearly worse off than I am. She notices that I'm feeling sorry for her, and says, "It's not so bad. It just wouldn't be right yet. I need to take some time. And while I do that, I'm keeping Olivia company. She likes having me here."

Our marriage is nonexistent. In this peculiar house, in these strange surroundings, Marianne seems strange as well. I shouldn't have come. There's nothing for me here. The anticipated intimacy of the double bed that we're standing beside doesn't suit us at all. I haven't the slightest desire to touch Marianne, and her body language tells me she'd crumble to ash if I did. Nonetheless I ask her, mostly in order to fulfill my role as loyal spouse, and without any serious intent, "Are you coming back?"

We look at each other, and after a while she slowly shakes her head. I'm almost relieved—at last, a straight answer. But then she says, "I need time. A lot of time."

I figure she should take as much time as she wants.

36

A quartet is about to entertain us with some chamber music. The musicians and their instruments have already taken their places in the corner. Olivia is greeting her guests, and the staff is keeping them supplied with aperitifs. The faces of the men and women to whom I am introduced, if I happen not to know them, are all old, radiant masks of lifelong social success. In one of the many mirrors that stand and hang all around this house, my eye chances to meet my reflection. I consider it for a moment as though looking at a stranger, and am surprised at how *good* I look. But I don't feel good at all. My professional failure, my shattered existence, you could call it, dulls my perception of myself. So it feels like an almost unbearably unearned distinction when the dean of the local business-management faculty amiably puts his arm around my shoulder and—clearly joking, certain that I will pass this little exam with flying colors—asks, "Well, my young friend? How's business?"

Or is his question one of sheer mockery? Surely he must know that Marianne moved in with Olivia only because of her own professional failure? So how does he see me? As a man who can't afford to keep his wife? Does he know I've been fired from the bank?

"Fine," I say, and my voice breaks. I clear my throat and repeat more clearly, "Fine," and continue in something of a mumble, "I've set up, um, on my own," and I clear my throat again.

The professor shakes my shoulder encouragingly.

"That's fantastic! And in what field? Our economy needs young risk-takers. A much-neglected quality!"

"Umm, consulting, you might say. Illegal steroids, drugs, money laundering—stuff like that."

The professor laughs long and loud and calls to Marianne, who is talking with another guest not far away: "Haha, Marianne! Your husband has a terrific sense of humor. Really terrific!"

Then he calms down and looks me steadily in the eye to hear the truth. Fine, I think, then let him hear the truth he wants to hear. The fact that he thinks my real life is a terrific joke actually makes me warm to him.

"Okay: I—I advise banks. I advise banks about complicated enforcement issues. I'm—it's all very secret."

Now I feel like laughing myself, but the professor clearly thinks what I'm saying is credible, even interesting. I say, "You know, in my view, the problem in our society lies in the fact that everyone's living on credit. Anyone like you or me, who earns his money honestly and spends only what he has, hasn't understood the system. In a word: Get what you can, and pay nothing back."

"Don't you think—forgive me—that's a rather simplistic view of things?"

Damn, that was too crass. I'd hoped I'd be able to establish some common ground by delivering a little sermon about the decline in contemporary payment practice, but he wouldn't hear of it. Perhaps he's got debts himself? I try making some remarks about the economic significance of debt. He nods politely, bored, barely listening to me. I break off midsentence and start a new one: "Of course I've got some customers who need special treatment. Secure accounts in Austria and Switzerland."

Apparently involuntarily, he frowns, turns his face to me with a jerk, and says, "Ah."

"Yes, yes. Of course," I say, head lowered.

"And you've got . . . ?"

"Contacts? The very best," I lie.

"And that must be very exciting, isn't it?"

"Very."

"And what sort of client base do you have?"

"Hard to say in a nutshell. But no, hang on: high earners. That's right, most of them come from the highest income bracket."

"How would you define those people?"

"Well, they're people who—who earn a lot. Don't you think? They earn more than other people, more than they have any right to expect, more than the tax office likes. I think it's absolutely legitimate for these people to try to achieve a proper reward for all their hard work."

The professor grins a broad grin. I finally seem to have come up with what he considers a stimulating conversation. The next logical step, of course, would be to offer to ferry his illegal earnings abroad. But I don't want to rush things, I've got quite enough problems already.

The professor and I bow respectfully to each other. I give him my card, and we find new people to talk to. It isn't long before Marianne introduces me to an art dealer who says she's very interested in meeting me, and who tells me right away that people in her line of business always get paid in cash these days. Olivia walks past us and whispers to me, "You are telling some very interesting stories. I'd like to talk to you."

I nod, almost embarrassed by my success. That evening I talk to about twenty or thirty rich people, all of them as discreet as possible in their own way, and making it clear to me that they want me to bring their money to Austria or Switzerland. Then we all listen to the chamber music.

While I then enthusiastically devote myself to the champagne, already seriously imagining new opportunities—it can't be that hard to find a way of opening a few anonymous numbered accounts in the Alps, with the help of Uwe and Anatol—sobriety follows hot on its heels.

And it's Marianne who supplies it. She's been studying my chattiness first with astonishment, then with suspicion. But now she sets about *maneuvering* me into the most embarrassing situations, by telling the people I've just been speaking to that I haven't got the kind of contacts you need to set up a numbered account. I notice that the people who, just a few minutes ago, were beaming at me with hope and anticipation are now, having spoken to Marianne, suddenly avoiding my eye, so I pull her somewhat roughly aside and hiss at her, "What are you saying to all these people!"

She hisses back, "What sort of crap are *you* coming out with? Can't you see that you're making a complete and utter idiot of yourself?"

"Oh, come on, I really *do* that thing with the numbered accounts. I *do* have contacts."

"*I* have to go on living with these people long after you're gone, and, more to the point, so does Olivia. Believe me, I'll make sure not one of them gives you so much as a mark."

She pulls her arm out of my clutches and leaves me standing there. So that's that. That's it. I should go now, but it would only make things worse. There's no point, there's really no point anymore. I try to vanish slowly into the crowd. When I find myself unnoticed near a door, I seize the opportunity and discreetly leave the room, without saying goodbye to anybody, of course.

37

Marianne didn't notice the finger marks on my throat. Not even when we said goodbye at the station. Our farewell was cool, but of course no final decisions were made about anything. As we waited for the train, we didn't talk much, we just frowned and smoked.

When I get home I forget my marital problems all at once. The lock to my apartment has been changed, and I can easily imagine who did that. I sit down on the stairs and smoke a cigarette. My first impulse, of course, is to march furiously across to Uwe and Anatol and have words with them. But that could be damaging to my health, no doubt about it. I've obviously got to go down and see them. But I've got to treat them as accomplices. They clearly couldn't give a damn. I mean, things like the inviolability of one's living space, other people's property, in the simplest possible terms: the private sphere. I've got some pretty awful ideas about what things look like behind the door to my flat.

Uwe and Anatol welcome me into their office with a kind of phony friendliness that frightens the life out of me. They apologize for any inconvenience I might have had with the lock, but I left without telling them, and they had to go ahead without asking me, and after all, they didn't know when I was coming back, and they could hardly keep their clients waiting.

And you can't, of course.

"And, um, am I getting—do I get a key? To *my* place, I mean?" I ask cautiously.

Of course, certainly, course you do, they reply, amused. They laugh a little. Then Uwe gets serious and says, "Listen up: We're not all that happy that you've turned up here today of all days. We thought you'd taken a well-deserved break for a bit. But now here you are. Fine. That means you're working for us again. And there's lots to be done."

He makes a dramatic pause and looks at me severely. I say nothing and wait for him to continue.

"Tonight at two, Uncle Doctor is coming with the medicine, and the handover's taking place in your flat. It's all set up. I've got the three hundred thousand and we're all ready. Afterward, to pass the time, we'll go to Funkadelic and have some fun. I'd suggest you come with us and keep us company."

"Of course I will. But I'd like to freshen up a bit, too. At my place. Is that okay?"

"Anatol will go with you."

So I'm really not going to get into my apartment on my own. That's fine, then. Anatol holds the key in front of my nose, and I'm about to take it when he pulls it away and walks in ahead of me.

They've taken great care to clear out the hall. And the living room. All the pictures and curtains have been removed, the windows have been sealed shut with black foil. I stand in the middle of the room, revolve slowly on my own axis, and shake my head, open-mouthed. After one complete revolution I quietly ask Anatol, "Please, please, please, Anatol. Just give me one, just one single sensible reason for all this crap. And most importantly, tell me: Where are my things?"

"Your things are all next door in your study. It's stacked up to the ceiling. Come on, get changed now."

"Um, Anatol—you didn't answer the most interesting part of the question."

Anatol grins and sends me into the bathroom with a nod of his head. I get fresh clothes out of the walk-in closet in the hall—they haven't touched that—and go off to freshen up.

It's still quite early when we arrive at the Funkadelic, just after nine. They're playing a kind of seventies psychedelic soul that goes

quite well with my mood and my suit. I'm not especially worried. I
am a bit, but not unpleasantly so. Things are just going to have to
take their course from now on, I'm sure of that. I feel almost the way
I did when I was still working for the bank—for example, if I was
facing a hard negotiation with one of my debtors. Just do what has
to be done, step by step, no distractions, and in the end you get the
result you're after.

Uwe and Anatol do their usual routine—their regular seats at
the back bar, Johnny Walker, talking big, showing off their muscles,
disappearing to the men's room, coking up.

Sabine comes. We greet each other as though we were a couple, we embrace and kiss. Uwe and Anatol look on, moderately
interested. I put my arm around Sabine's shoulders and whisper in
her ear, "Are you coming?"

"Where to?"

"The dance floor?"

She nods, we go over and dance for a bit. The dance floor is
still empty, no one apart from us is dancing. I watch her dancing.
She's a nice mover, sexy. I think to myself, Okay, why not let her in
on it.

On the way back to the bar I say to her, "If you feel like taking
a little trip with me, let's meet up here outside the Funkadelic at four
o'clock in the morning."

She looks at me quizzically and with, I assume, a serious expression that's supposed to mean: No questions. She understands.
And nods! I ask, just to be sure, "You'll be there?"

She nods again. It's cool.

I spend some time hanging out at the bar with Sabine, and
when Uwe and Anatol join us, I give them a sign to tell them I'm
going to the men's room to do a line. They shake their heads to
indicate that they've just been there, so I go on my own. There's a
phone beside the toilet door, and I dial Bellmann's private number.

"Hi, Schwarz here."

"Schwarz? What do you want?"

"I've been working hard."

"What's that supposed to mean?"

"It's supposed to mean: I now know that Uwe and Anatol are front men for Furnituro Ltd."

"Proof?"

"Me. I'm your witness. They've told me themselves. They've told me the tiniest, most microscopic details about how their business works, who's involved, and so on. I've got names, I've got information, I know everything you need to know if you're going to seize their property."

"And I'm supposed to believe this?"

"Fine, if you don't, forget it."

"I do, I do! Just asking. So what should we do?"

"Get hold of a search warrant, a bailiff, and a few hard men. And then come to the fitness studio at exactly a quarter past two. Quarter past two, you hear me? Not a minute earlier, not a minute later. Uwe, Anatol, and presumably a few other characters, self included, will be there. You can impound whatever you want. Appliances, machines, furniture, cashbox, safe, everything."

"And what about you?"

"They think I'm with them. As soon as you show up and do your job, I'm off. Your people have to make sure I can get to the door. That's my only condition. Apart from keeping to our agreement, of course."

"What's that?"

"If that doesn't happen, I'm not your witness. And of course I'm not your witness if you rat on me, either. I'm going to be personally ratting out Uwe and Anatol in the courtroom. Not a word from you beforehand, you hear? If you make one mistake or give me away, I've forgotten everything I ever knew."

"And what are you going to do?"

"I'm taking a trip for a while until the case quiets down a bit."

"I'll be there at two."

"For God's sake, no, Bellmann. Quarter past two. Quarter past two. If you come any earlier you're going to screw everything up. Okay?"

"Okay, quarter past two."

I hang up. When I get back to the bar, Uwe says I shouldn't overdo the coke, we've got stuff to do tonight. "What kind of stuff?" I shout cheerfully, grabbing Sabine to go dancing again. I haven't felt this loose-hipped for ages.

38

The white, unfiltered light in the office of the fitness studio doesn't do much for our looks. Anatol's nostrils are surrounded by two inflamed red rings, the bluish-brownish circles under his eyes reach his cheekbones. He stares at the ceiling, mouth half open, his bronchia rattling with each breath he takes. Uwe's eyes are as red as a pair of cherries, he keeps rubbing them as he counts out the bills on the desk. There are three hundred rolls of ten one-hundred-mark notes. Uncle Doctor will be here in an hour. I ask Uwe, "Is it right?"

"It's right, it's right. I've got nothing to put it in. What could we put it in?"

I'm surprised at how nervous the guys are. It's their job, after all. I'm getting quite worked up, too. But then it's my balls that are on the line, whereas for them it's just their business. Big difference. I say, "I've got one of those Samsonite cases upstairs. It's small, just a little thing for hand luggage on the plane. It would fit perfectly."

Uwe studies me thoughtfully. Then he says to Anatol, "Go and get it."

We go up to my place and get the case. There's a "T" stuck on the left-hand lock, and an "S" on the one on the right—my initials. I ask Uwe, "Is that a problem?"

Uwe has a think, and asks me, "Are the initials a problem for you?"

"Not for me."

Uwe packs the money into the case, shuts it, and puts it on the floor beside the desk.

"I'll mess up the combination. Uncle Doctor's sure to find a way of getting the thing open."

I don't know what objection there could be to actually *telling* the doctor the combination, but I keep my mouth shut.

We wait.

The three of us walk up and down in various directions around the fitness studio, chain-smoking. After each cigarette that Uwe stubs out in a saucer on the desk, he says in disgust, "Fucking smoke."

As I walk up and down, smoking, smoking, smoking, I gradually have a sense of what it means to be *scared shitless*, and feel a terrible need for regret. But what have I to regret? I regret the fact that I'm in danger, insofar as you can regret something like that. What if Bellmann comes running in before Uncle Doctor shows up? Was I clear enough when I told him not to come a minute later than a quarter past two? I think so. But what if Uncle Doctor's late? What if Bellmann can't wait and simply comes storming in here? Then Uwe will kill me. There's no doubt about that. I try to think up some excuses for that eventuality. But while I'm walking up and down in this unhealthy neon light, I clearly have the impression that my brain consists entirely of stirred-up shit. So: smoke, smoke, smoke until the doorbell rings.

It rings.

All three of us stop and look at one another in terror, as though this is something unexpected, as though it isn't exactly what we've been waiting for. Uwe keeps his composure. He takes a blackjack— an elegant little steel rod with a hard rubber joint above the shaft— out of his desk drawer and walks over to the door, which Anatol and I can't see from where we're standing. Uwe brings in a man who isn't Bellmann and doesn't look like a hard man. He's on his own, so this must be Uncle Doctor. I don't quite trust my conclusions, but I sense an almost ludicrous degree of relief when Uwe says, "Sit down, Doctor."

The man indicates that he doesn't want to sit down. He has a fine, hard, arrogant face. He says, "My colleagues are in the car with the goods. I don't want to waste any time. Where do we start?"

"We've set up a place where we can do the handover, and where we can examine the quality of the goods in peace, and deal with the payment," Uwe says, now fairly relaxed.

"Can my people come, too?"

"Of course. But they'll have to wear blindfolds, like you."

I'm more excited, I think, than I've ever been in my life, but at the idea of the doctor and his "people" stumbling up into my and Marianne's place with blindfolds on, I get a fit of the giggles. I splutter away more or less hysterically, and everyone looks at me with expressions of fury and menace. I calm down again, but it's not easy.

The doctor has agreed to the blindfolds. Maybe he sees it as a sign of gangster professionalism. He asks if he can make a call. A call? Now? A lot of fuss, a lot of excitement. He wants to call on his cell phone. Ah, okay then, his cell phone, that's different, but just one conversation and only a short one at that. The doctor dials a number, listens, says strictly, "Come in!," switches it off, and puts it away again.

There's a ring, at the door. I feel gasoline in my veins. Bellmann? Or the doctor's "people"? Uwe looks at me and points toward the door, relaxed, almost friendly. I walk over and open up. Who's standing in front of me? It's still not Bellmann. Two men. The doctor's "people," no doubt about it. They look as you might expect. Fairly young, fairly hesitant, with an indisputably negative aura. I'm happy, almost. Now we're all here. Now Bellmann can come running in with his crowd and the party can begin.

Uwe greets the doctor's two jumpy henchmen with a handshake. He asks, "Where's the goods?"

The doctor gives a pinched smile and replies, "Where's the money?"

"As I said, the handover will occur in a room set up for the purpose. That's what you stipulated, Doctor. And it's fine by me. If we carry out the handover there, you won't be able to tell anyone where it happened—even if you wanted to. But: Who's going to bring in the goods?"

I can't figure out the rigamarole they're going through. Why not just goods in, money out, and have done with it? Of course they're all scared. They're all crapping themselves. Are the doctor and his people armed? Are Uwe and Anatol carrying guns? Is the plan for them all to shoot one another, or are they going to make some sort of deal?

I whisper to Anatol, who's standing next to me, "What's the problem, for God's sake?"

He growls, "Keep your trap shut, or you'll be the problem. Uwe's taking his time. He wants to get to know who he's doing business with. It's all tactics."

The doorbell rings.

39

Nobody moves, nobody makes a sound. Nobody has a tactic for this. The doorbell rings again. Beyond any doubt, there's someone at the door who'd like to be let in. I know who it is, and I'm still as surprised as everyone else.

This time Anatol is sent to open the door. When he does, things get noisy. Men's voices yelling. Bellmann's coming. He marches into the office with a kind of goose step. Behind him is Anatol, with Schmidt the bailiff clutching him by the arm. Schmidt is waving a piece of paper around in the air. Behind Schmidt are four men I don't know. Men in coal-black suits with department-store ties around their bull necks and close-shaven hair. Uwe stands up. Bellmann shouts, "Sit right where you are!"

For a moment Uwe isn't sure what to do. Then he sits down again and beckons me over. Bellmann shouts, "We're clearing this place out!"

He walks up to Uwe: "You wanted to break the bank, did you? And now the bank's breaking you."

Uwe tries to stay cool: "I don't know what you're talking about. I owe you nothing. My partners owe you nothing. And you're trespassing."

Bellmann laughs sardonically and turns to his people: "Let's start searching this place systematically and clearing it out."

He gives instructions about who's to search what. In the meantime I've walked over to Uwe. He whispers to me, "Listen, my friend. I hope you don't have anything to do with this shit. If I ever find out you did—I'll kill you. And I mean it."

The way he looks at me, I believe he does mean it. He goes

on: "You're the only one of us they're going to let go without a fuss. So take the case and say it's got your things in it if he asks you. And bring it back tomorrow. I swear to you, if one single note is missing, I'm going to beat you to a pulp."

I nod. Bellmann bellows in our direction, "What are you two talking about?"

I clear my throat, stand up, pick up the case. Bellmann looks at me, waiting for an explanation. I say, "I have nothing to do with all this. I'd like to go."

"No one's stopping you. Is that your case?"

"Yes, it's my case. I'm going away for a while, and I was just saying goodbye to my neighbors here."

Bellmann waves me on like a traffic cop. I was planning on showing him the initials on the case—*my* initials. But he hasn't the slightest interest in me. So I stroll straight out of the fitness studio. At the door I hear Herr Doctor awkwardly explaining that he really has to go, too. I think to myself, Just stand up and go, then, they can't do anything to you . . .

I can hardly believe it when I close the door behind me. I just walked out with a case containing three hundred thousand marks, which are from this moment all at my disposal. I just have to stay calm.

I run down into the underground parking lot and jump into my Subaru. I drive to the Funkadelic. I have to be careful to drive slowly, I have to be sure that no one's after me, or at least not for the moment. Bellmann is going to do over the whole of the fitness studio and the whole of Period Furniture Paradise. That'll take at least two hours. Then they'll clear out everything that's worth anything at all. That'll take another two hours, at least. By then I'll be miles away, over the border. Of course Uwe and Anatol don't have the slightest notion where I'm going. It would be even safer for me to travel without Sabine. She could still rat me out to the others. But she won't do that as long as I have the money. And I don't want to miss out on the fun of taking my little trip, the one I've planned, with a pretty woman at my side.

I arrive at the Funkadelic and park right outside the front door. I realize you can get away with that kind of thing only if you're driving a Jaguar, a Rolls, or at least a Mercedes, but I can't get hung up on details like that right now. I walk up the steps to the front door, and the bouncer, who knows I'm a friend of Uwe, welcomes me with a sleazy grin.

"Nice wheels."

"It's a Subaru. You wouldn't believe what it's got under the hood. When I've got a little more time, I'll let you have the keys."

He laughs with genuine disgust. I ask him, "Have you seen Sabine?"

"She's on the dance floor. Having fun, by the look of it."

I walk in, order a whisky and Coke from one of the waiters walking about, and peer across the dance floor from the edge. I know the music: James Brown.

And sure enough, there's Sabine, dancing and draped around some guy who certainly doesn't drive a Subaru: a paunchy guy in a double-breasted suit with a hanky sticking out of his top pocket. I walk over and tap him on the shoulder. He doesn't react. Again, a bit harder. He lets go of Sabine and turns around to me: "What do you want?"

"To pick up my girlfriend," I say.

He steps aside, flabbergasted. I turn to Sabine. "Would you like to come to Monaco for a few days?"

"To where?"

"Monaco. Spend some money."

Sabine looks around. The guy with the hanky has wandered off. Then she looks at me again and says, "Why not?"

40

But what, I ask you, is three hundred thousand when you've got a presumably very, very bad-tempered gorilla like Uwe on your heels? Not a lot, you're right. Or more precisely: nothing at all. If you've got thirty-six times three hundred thousand, things start to look a little different. Don't they? How much would that be? Correct: ten point eight million. I haven't done the precise calculation yet, but I think that would be me pretty well looked after for the next hundred years, at least.

The plan: I drive to Monaco with Sabine, walk into the casino, and put all the money on zero. And if I win, I'll be ten million five hundred thousand marks richer. Pretty good, don't you think? Of course you do! And so do I.

The truth is that I haven't been able to stop giggling since I've been sitting in my Subaru with Sabine, bombing toward Monaco at a hundred miles an hour. That's how fast he goes, my bold little Jap, believe it or not. I'm chain-smoking, and Sabine isn't entirely at ease.

"So what are we up to now?" she asks cautiously.

She really is charming, don't you think? What am I up to? I'm not all that sure myself. To put her at her ease. I say, "I want to take a little holiday with you."

I don't want to let her in on all the details, not at first. She'd just be scared. The radio's on, the traffic station says: there are no traffic problems to report. The news: nothing about what happened tonight. And there won't be anything about it tomorrow, either. The thing that happened doesn't belong on the radio. I haven't robbed a bank, or whatever. Nonetheless I switch on the news channel every quarter of the hour. Nothing. I should be happy, really. What do you mean "should"? I *am* happy.

It's early morning when we cross the border into Italy. A clear sky—looks like the weather's going to be good. The highways are empty, and we dash at top speed toward Liguria. Road signs tell us that we're driving through Lombardy. I dimly remember that this is some sort of historical region. But the highways leading through it are dead straight; you can see nothing but meadows and fields, nothing that would unsettle you or distract you from driving. I feel just as I would if I were driving through the Siberian steppes.

Sabine has gone to sleep. She's lowered the passenger seat, her face is turned toward me, her mouth half open. She looks more relaxed than I've ever seen her before. I light another cigarette. I'm not even slightly tired, which probably has something to do with the fact that my body has produced more adrenaline in the last twelve hours than in the whole of the previous thirty-five years.

However hard I try, I can't imagine the coming evening at the casino. And I really don't have to. We'll arrive in Monaco and check in at an exquisite hotel opposite the casino. I mean, there's got to be one—an exquisite hotel opposite the casino. Of course there does. I figure we'll get there at about midday. A suite, please, with a view of the Côte d'Azur and an extra-large bathtub, if that can be arranged. Is that okay? Thank you. I will take a long bath with Sabine and a bottle of champagne, and then fuck her in peace. After that we'll get room service to send us up some snacks and then we'll sleep for a while. We'll go out early in the evening to buy some clothes at one of the very best boutiques. There'll be dozens of them, selling the most exquisite couture in either the hotel or somewhere nearby. I'll put on a smoking jacket, the first I've ever had. And Sabine will get a dress that will make everyone in the casino think she's a film star or an American billionairess. At least. We'll get back to our suite and get ourselves ready for the evening. I'll get one of the hotel lackeys who do that kind of thing—they must have them,

I hope they do!—to tie my bow tie, because I don't know how to. Sabine will put on the extraordinary perfume that I've just given her. We will look at ourselves in the floor-to-ceiling baroque mirror in our suite, and agree that we look like a royal couple, specially invented for the tabloid press. I will go to the phone and order a Pullman limo from reception. A white one, please, if possible, monsieur. We will climb into the car, and zealously helpful staff will eye Sabine's dress.

We will drive the hundred yards to the casino in the limo, which will roll up in front of the imposing entrance. The staff there will run forward with the expected degree of humility and open the doors for us. We'll get out, with the triumphant smiles of future royalty on our faces. We will step through enormous doors and halls, past the curious and admiring faces of everyone present. I will buy chips. As casually as anyone could imagine, I will buy chips, three hundred thousand marks' worth. Then we'll find ourselves a gaming table. The one with the most players sitting around it. At the next game we'll put the maximum on zero. Always on zero. What's the maximum in Monte Carlo? Ten thousand? Twenty thousand? Whatever. We'll bet on zero. All evening. Until the three hundred thousand's all gone. Then we'll leave the halls with the same regal smile we came in with.

Is that what'll happen? I'm afraid Sabine won't play. At least not with the second part of my plan, plan zero. She'll think I'm crazy, she'll think I'm insane, and she'll ruin everything by bawling her eyes out. Who cares? Of course we could just go on living in one of those suites until the money ran out. One way or another it should be possible to get through three hundred thousand marks in Monaco within a reasonable space of time. I'm sure of that, and that's why I have to get to Monaco. And once the money's gone, Sabine'll be gone, too. That's why it was Sabine I wanted here, not Marianne. Once the money and Sabine have gone,

I won't have the slightest chance of getting back on my feet in Monaco. No one knows me there, and they won't want to know anyone with no money. And in the end that's why this will be the easiest place in the world for me to rid myself of something I've never had, anyway: an identity.